BIG BAD

WHITNEY COLLINS

SARABANDE BOOKS

Louisville, KY

Library of Congress Cataloging-in-Publication Data

Names: Collins, Whitney, MFA, author.
Title: Big bad : stories / by Whitney Collins.
Description: First edition. | Louisville, KY : Sarabande Books, 2021
Identifiers: LCCN 2020016783 (print) | LCCN 2020016784 (e-book)
ISBN 9781946448729 (paperback) | ISBN 9781946448736 (e-book)
Subjects: LCGFT: Short stories.
Classification: LCC PS3603.O45633 B55 2021 (print)
LCC PS3603.O45633 (e-book) | DDC 813/.6—dc23
LC record available at https://lccn.loc.gov/2020016783
LC ebook record available at https://lccn.loc.gov/2020016784

Cover and interior design by Alban Fischer.
Printed in Canada.
This book is printed on acid-free paper.
Sarabande Books is a nonprofit literary organization.

This project is supported in part by an award from the National
Endowment for the Arts. The Kentucky Arts Council, the state arts
agency, supports Sarabande Books with state tax dollars and federal
funding from the National Endowment for the Arts.

for my sons, my suns

CONTENTS

You save yourself or you remain unsaved.

—ALICE SEBOLD

THE NEST

O N TUESDAY, FRANKIE'S father took her two places against his better judgment. The first was to see her premature brothers at the Our Lady of Peace NICU. Three days prior, and sixty days too early, James and Jasper had slipped out of Frankie's mother like a pair of feeble insects that doctors promptly secured under glass for observation both scientific and sacred. In the ensuing emergency, Frankie's father, unable to locate a sitter, deposited his six-year-old daughter on the foot of his blind mother's nursing home bed with a naked baby doll and a box of Sun-Maid raisins.

For two days, Frankie watched *The Young and the Restless* and *Who Wants to Be a Millionaire?* from a vinyl recliner, eating saltines and applesauce and drinking Boost, while her grandmother's friends leaned on walkers in the doorway, admiring her like a misplaced peacock. "She's a prodigy," the grandmother claimed. "She's in first grade and can balance a checkbook. She knows all the Canadian provinces."

Every so often, the grandmother would run her fingers over Frankie's soft face, as if her eyebrows were made of Braille, and tell her the baby brothers would probably die. "They're like worms on

1

a summer sidewalk, child. They don't stand a chance in the heat of this world." To Frankie, this honesty felt so much like affection, she sometimes asked her grandmother to repeat herself, which the grandmother did with gusto, adding details about Frankie's father and her Uncle Eric. How they weren't born early, but they'd been stuck together at the hip and the doctors had to slice the grandmother open to remove them. "I was the one who almost died," she said. "Those boys were laying inside me, side by side, like a butterfly. Your father. He got the hip. Eric, he never was right." At this, the grandmother patted Frankie's face and body with her hands. "Looks like you'll make it," she said. "You're one of the lucky ones." Then Frankie, full of herself, excused herself to faux tap-dance in the hallway for nickels, making four dollars in one commercial break— enough to buy just one brother something in the hospital gift shop.

Back in the recliner, Frankie covered herself with an afghan that smelled of menthol. She saw that her grandmother was on the verge of sleep, so she asked, "Did it hurt when they pulled the babies out of you?"

Her grandmother jolted, frowned, then nodded. "It was hell," she quietly moaned. "Oh, child. Let me tell you: I know hell."

Frankie thought about this in the dark, while the mute television featured a man selling electric grills that nothing stuck to, not even cheese. Frankie knew a little about hell. About how, in October, she'd turn seven. How then she'd be considered responsible for everything she did and everything she thought. How the week before Halloween, Father Greg would be waiting for her and her classmates in the church booth to tell him everything they had ever done wrong.

Frankie had already started the list in her mind. She had stolen a pack of Juicy Fruit from the drugstore when she was four. She had dropped one of her mother's diamond earrings down the drain (on accident) and never told (on purpose) when she was five. And once, just a month ago, when her mother was too pregnant to get off the park bench, Frankie had come across a boy inside the playground tunnel beating a rock against a limp chipmunk. When he offered her a turn, she said okay, but made the mistake of wrapping her hand completely around the rock so that when she hit the chipmunk, her knuckles could feel its bones break, could feel how it was still warm. Frankie had decided to only mention the gum to Father Greg, which would be another sin. The more Frankie thought about it, the more she couldn't see a way to keep herself out of hell. But she fell asleep regardless.

On Tuesday, the nursing home manager came to the grandmother's room. He stood in the doorway and explained that Frankie, by law, had to leave. Frankie gathered up her things, but not before noticing that the toes of the man's shoes were wrapped in black tape to hold the soles on. In his office, he called her father and said, "Either you or the police can come pick her up."

*

Last November, to everyone's surprise, Uncle Eric called to invite Frankie and her parents to Thanksgiving dinner at his house.

"He says your mother will be there with her nurse," Frankie's mother said to Frankie's father. "Maybe he's finally trying."

"Right," her father said. "Don't hold your breath."

On the day of the party, Frankie's mother dressed Frankie in her brown, sashed dress and her gray wool coat with the brass buttons. Frankie had only met her uncle once before, at her grandfather's funeral. She remembered he'd stood under a pine tree away from the crowd, holding an umbrella even though it wasn't raining.

"Will any kids be there?" Frankie asked.

"No," her mother said. "Just you."

When they arrived at his house, Frankie could barely contain herself. The bungalow was painted bright purple with an orange front door, and on the roof, attached to the chimney with duct tape, was a faded plastic Santa Claus.

"Jesus," her father sighed.

"David," her mother said.

For dinner, instead of turkey and stuffing and a normal-sized pumpkin pie that fed eight people, Eric served each guest a tiny roasted quail, and minuscule mounds of sweet potatoes scooped with a melon baller, and dwarfed apple tarts the size of poker chips. In her whole young life, Frankie had never been so delighted. There were ropes of blue tinsel over every doorway and glitter sprinkled on the tablecloth and six strangers at the meal who were of no relation to Frankie or her parents or her blind grandmother, but who loved on Frankie more than she'd ever been loved on before—strangers who looked like women but talked like men and smoked cigarettes as long as chopsticks and cried every time a song came on the radio.

"The dishes," Eric announced at dinner, pinching up a teacup for everyone to see, "are antique doll's china from Russia."

Frankie inspected her plate with awe. The dinner guests, the ones who weren't family, gasped.

"They belonged to Anna Rasputin," Uncle Eric said. "Anna Goddamn Rasputin. That's how much I love you all."

Frankie ate four apple tarts and eleven scoops of sweet potatoes. Her quail was so precious she wrapped it in her napkin then excused herself to the bathroom. She found her winter coat in the hallway and placed the bird in its inner silk pocket.

Frankie noticed her father did not eat. Frankie noticed her grandmother's nurse excused the grandmother from the dining table and fed her from a paper plate in the living room. Frankie noticed her mother spent the whole meal watching Frankie's father in the same way she watched Frankie when she ran a fever. Frankie noticed Uncle Eric noticed none of this.

After dinner, Uncle Eric took Frankie upstairs to his bedroom where he showed her a red toddler-sized piano. "We must bring this downstairs," he said, flushed and wide-eyed. "We've got to keep the teeny-tiny theme going." Frankie nodded in agreement. "What do you play, Frankie? *Für Elise*? Please tell me you play *Für Elise*."

Frankie was worried; she only knew "The Mayflower Song." "I only know 'The Mayflower Song,'" she said.

"That's perfect!" Uncle Eric said, placing the piano on the shoulder opposite his cane. "Because guess who invented Thanksgiving, Sugar? The motherfucking Pilgrims, that's who."

On their way downstairs with the piano, Frankie and Uncle Eric met Frankie's father on his way upstairs. "It's time to go, Frankie. Your mother is waiting on the porch."

Uncle Eric stomped a foot. "You're leaving?" he huffed. "But Frankie was just going to play us a song."

Frankie's father shook his head. "Frankie will not be participating in your circus, Eric."

"Circus?" Uncle Eric exclaimed. "That's what you call this?" Uncle Eric waved his cane in all directions. "I spent six days getting this ready. Do you know how hard it was to find twelve quail that would fit on that china? I took one of Anna Rasputin's doll plates around to four butchers and then a farm. Four butchers and a farm, David."

Frankie stood and watched. Uncle Eric's blue eyelids looked

heavy. Her father had his feet on two different steps as if he might pounce. "Why can't you just do things the regular way?" her father said. "Why couldn't there have been a normal turkey? And why all these people, Eric? Answer me that." Uncle Eric patted his pockets with the crook of his cane. Frankie knew he was looking for a cigarette. "I'll tell you why," her father continued. "It's because it's never about anybody but you. It's about what *you* want. It's about drawing attention to yourself. It's not about Thanksgiving or family. It's about Eric. The Eric Show."

Frankie looked at her uncle. She wondered what he might say. How he might make her father feel terrible for what he'd just done. But Uncle Eric said nothing. He simply lifted the toy piano off his shoulder and into the air with one hand and then threw the piano down the stairs, over Frankie's father's head and onto the first-floor landing, where it jangled and splintered in a way that almost made Frankie laugh. It was exciting to see her father scared, even for a flash. Frankie's father reached up and yanked her down by her dress sash to the step his back foot was on. Uncle Eric pulled out a pack of Viceroys and pointed at his brother. "Get the fuck out," he said. "And Frankie? I love you."

On the ride home, Frankie's mother and father were silent. Neither of them moved, not one millimeter. It was as if the car drove itself. In the backseat, Frankie sat, replaying the piano scene. Up it went, her father cringed, down it came, exploding in a plinking pile. Frankie smiled wide in the dark in her brass-buttoned coat. She placed her hand over the lump that was the hidden quail.

*

When Frankie's mother saw her in the doorway of her hospital room, she succumbed to a spasm of sobs that Frankie at first mistook for uncontrollable laughter and that her father, quite clearly, had grown accustomed to. Maybe even tired of.

"Frankie is here, Catherine," her father said, as if reintroducing them at a dinner party. "She's come to see her brothers."

Frankie's mother convulsed in the wheelchair on the way to the NICU. "They're . . . ," she struggled, "so tiny, Frankie. Say a prayer," she choked. "Oh, God. Say your prayers."

Frankie was revulsed by her mother's brokenness, by her desperate pleas for the pointless type of prayers that had no beginning or end. She touched her mother's hair absentmindedly to pretend she was not appalled, but her curiosity over James and Jasper outweighed her compassion, and she tried to make up for this by showing her mother the fringe of her socks. Frankie did not like fringed socks, but her grandmother had insisted she dress as if for a recital. On Monday, her grandmother had sent an orderly out to buy a pair of patent leather shoes and dress socks on her lunch break, and Frankie had been instructed to go to the grandmother's jewelry box and give the orderly a gold watch for her efforts.

"See my socks?" Frankie said, smiling, looking past her mother's contorted face. "See my shoes?" *Where were these brothers?* was what Frankie really wondered. *How terrifying would they be?*

To Frankie's delight, they were horrendous. Beetles under bell jars. Featherless starlings fallen from a nest. Their skin red and shiny, their matchstick arms like roasted chicken wings stretched out to reveal pitiful armpits, their closed eyes bulbous and alien. Nurses turned them this way and that way with latex gloves, adjusting the tape and tubes and gaping diapers, but nothing made them look better or better off. When Frankie watched them, she imagined all the times she had twisted a coin in a candy machine only to forget to cup her hands under the silver spout.

She remembered all the times a gumball had escaped her, rolling under the desk at a car wash or on the tarry carpet of an old restaurant. All the times she had been forced to beg for a second quarter. And now, see? Her mother would have to ask for two. Frankie watched her brothers breathe, their tiny ribcages pumping to the beat of a frantic song. *Scary, scary, scary. Very, very, very.* Frankie could tell one of them was worse off than the other—Jasper it seemed from the sign on his little greenhouse. Frankie decided to root for him. *Go, Jasper,* she thought. *Beat James.* She knew this was terrible and she bent down to check that the lace of her socks was still folded neatly.

"I know it's hard to believe," her father said unconvincingly. "But one day your brothers will grow up to be big and strong. Bigger and stronger than you."

Frankie was done looking at them. She tapped her new shoes against the tile floor of the hospital hallway to show her parents she was the same as she had always been. "Can I go to the gift shop?" Frankie asked. "I have four dollars."

Her father nodded, and after they wheeled Frankie's mother back to her room, downstairs, in the hospital store, Frankie bought a tiny blue T-shirt that said *Early Bird.*

"Who's that for?" her father asked.

Frankie put it on her naked doll as they walked to the car in the heavy August heat. *Go, Jasper,* she thought. *Beat James.* "It's for my baby," she said.

*

The second place Frankie's father took her that day against his will was to his brother's, back to the Thanksgiving neighborhood where rainbow windsocks blew horizontal from porches.

"If I had my way . . . ," her father began, as he searched for a parking spot.

"You'd rather take me to the zoo," Frankie finished for him. "Why don't you go back to the hospital?" She changed the subject. "Before something bad happens."

Frankie's father slouched at the wheel, and she felt a small surge of victory in her stomach. "You can just drop me off," she said. "I know which house is his."

But her father parked and walked her up the stairs to the purple bungalow where Uncle Eric met them on the porch. He wore a silk bathrobe and a pair of red velvet slippers. He held an unlit cigarette and a new, jaunty magician's cane in one hand and placed his other hand on top of Frankie's head. "We're going to have a big time," he said. "You and me, Sugar. A grand old time."

Frankie left the men on the porch and went inside to snoop. She overheard her father say, low and tense, "Don't pull any of your shit."

In Uncle Eric's living room, Frankie watched a working stoplight in the corner cycle through its red-yellow-green. In his downstairs bathroom, she saw that the toilet water was blue. She flushed it once to see if it was blue again and it was and she was thrilled. In the kitchen, in the refrigerator, Frankie found a pink cake with one slice missing. "Happy Tuesday —itch," Frankie said aloud, with her hands on her hips.

"I ate the *W*," Uncle Eric confessed from the doorway. "And it was delicious."

Frankie turned. She suddenly felt shy but refused to show it. "My brothers will probably die," she said. "They're like two worms in the sun."

Uncle Eric snorted, shocked. "Gurrrrrl," he purred, fumbling through the pocket of his robe. "Go on, now. Tell us how you really feel." He produced a lighter and lit his cigarette and looked hard into Frankie's eyes when he exhaled.

"It's true," she said. "I've seen them. They're probably dead right now."

Uncle Eric shook his head admiringly. "I doubt that, Hon. What with modern medicine and all. But still." He shuffled to the refrigerator with his cane and brought out the cake, from which he cut a slice. He served it to Frankie on a paper towel at the chrome table. "I bet they looked bad off." He sat down across from Frankie with an amber ashtray and a coffee mug shaped like a woman's breast. "Didn't anybody tell you the story of your dad's and my birth? Everybody thought we wouldn't make it. And now, see? Look." Uncle Eric tilted his head back like a supermodel and puckered his lips. He rapped his cane on the floor three times. "They were right about one of us." At this, Eric laughed long and hard, and Frankie could tell he expected her to do the same. Eric pointed to her cake and then at her. "Oh, I'm just playing, Doll." He crushed out his cigarette and winked. "Now, you eat that, and then I want to show you something."

*

In the grandmother's jewelry box, next to the gold watch, Frankie had found a tarnished silver locket, as dark as if it had been dropped into a fire, as black as the lung the doctor had held up on television to warn children against smoking. Inside the locket, on the right side, was a small round picture of Frankie's father when he was about her age, which Frankie could not imagine had ever been the case, but there it was: photographic proof. On the left side of the locket, there was a tiny dot of glue and a white flake of photo paper. Uncle Eric was missing, having fallen off, Frankie guessed, after years of having a blind woman rake her hands over him. But as her grandmother dozed and Frankie messed through the giant synthetic pearls and tangles of brassy chains, Uncle Eric's round face appeared, ghostly, inside a tiny cellophane envelope, an insect's wing among scrap metal. From what Frankie could gather, Uncle Eric had been removed and relocated with intention, plucked off by her grandmother's thick, clouded fingernails.

Frankie thought of this as Uncle Eric brought out his dress. It was a floor-length gown with a mermaid cut, made of thousands of red feathers. On his shoulders he wore a sequined red, blue, and yellow cape that he could slide his arms into and spread like wings. "I'm a scarlet macaw," he said. "I'm thinking I should make a hood for it. To go over my head. With a beak and all."

Frankie was mesmerized. "What's it for?" she asked her uncle. "Where will you wear it?"

Eric leaned on his cane. "My show, Sugar," he said. "I wear it and I sing the song 'Somebody, Somewhere' by Loretta Lynn. You know Loretta, Sweetheart?"

Frankie shook her head. She wasn't interested in the song part. "Where's your nest?" she asked. "Every bird needs a nest."

Eric stopped and said nothing. He was thinking. "A nest," he whispered, his eyes darting around the room as if collecting supplies. "You mean, like an origin story?"

"No," Frankie said. "Like a nest."

Uncle Eric leaned forward on his cane, his long fingers curled over the crook like a parrot grasping its perch. "You want to know where I came from? I dream it all the time. I've had the same dream for thirty-eight years."

Frankie thought of her grandmother. "Your mother?"

Eric rolled his eyes. "Oh, Sister, please. Air France. I have this dream I'm on an Air France plane. Except it's not so much a plane as it is a saucer. It's like an Air France UFO. And I'm flying on it with hundreds and hundreds of other people. At this point, I've had the dream so many times, I've started to recognize these people. To anticipate them. They're decent, I guess. But I can't find any common denominator. We're not all trannies. We're not all Americans. But there we are: on an Air France UFO flying from Charles de Gaulle to fucking—sorry, *freaking*—Atlanta."

Frankie frowned. "That's how you got here?"

Eric nodded, fumbling through his robe pockets for his lighter and Viceroys. "Yep." He produced a cigarette, which seemed to bring him the same sort of relief Frankie'd felt when her father had said it was time to leave the hospital. "So. Where did you come from?"

Frankie thought for a moment. "My parents went down to the train station and showed the conductor a ticket. Like the kind you show the butcher when you wait in line for a roast."

Eric exhaled rapidly in approval. "And?"

"He gave them a suitcase and I was in it." Frankie thought some more. "I looked pretty good to them until a few years later. That was when they started going down to the train station for another baby, but the suitcases they kept picking up were empty. Then I didn't look so great anymore. It was like when you look at a word for a really long time and it stops making sense."

"Oh, this is good, Dollbaby."

"And they just kept going down to the train station with their butcher ticket until finally the conductor got tired of them and to make them go away he gave them a suitcase out of the lost and found." Frankie folded her arms and shook her head as if she stood on the sidelines of a playing field, watching a losing team. "The suitcase had two babies in it, but they'd been in lost and found for a long time and didn't look so good."

Uncle Eric looked like he was going to cry. "Oh, Princess," he sniffed. "You're an old soul, you know that?"

Frankie thought for a moment. Uncle Eric smoked and flapped his cape. "Where do you think babies go when they die? Back to the train station?"

Uncle Eric sat on the edge of his bed. He tapped his cigarette out on the bottom of his slipper, and Frankie watched the red ashes fall to the braided rug and die. Then he lit a second cigarette and Frankie thought of his lungs, a black, tarnished locket open in his chest. "I don't know where babies go when they die," he said. "I don't know where grown-ups go."

Frankie stood and assessed Uncle Eric's bedroom. She began with a quilt, which she placed in the center of the round braided rug, and she made it into the base of a nest. Then she went looking for other things in his drawers and closet: a towel, a second silk robe, a set of paisley sheets. "In October I have my first reconciliation," she said. "I have to tell Father Greg all the things I've ever done wrong. Then in April, I take Communion. That means from then on, if I die, I go to hell if I'm not sorry."

Eric exhaled and shook his head and rapped out his second cigarette on his slipper with such intent that Frankie thought the rug or his shoe might catch on fire. "Oh, Jesus H. Christ," he said. "No seven-year-old is going to hell."

Frankie shrugged. "It wouldn't scare me," she said. "I might even like it."

Uncle Eric bowed his head. "You and me both. I wouldn't know a damn soul in heaven anyway." He reached out to hug Frankie and she let him, but she kept her arms at her side. She wanted to hug him back, but then, when her father came to take her home, she'd be devastated.

"Let's make the nest," she said.

"Yes," Uncle Eric said, clapping his hands together once. "Let's."

Frankie and Uncle Eric gathered all the clothes and towels and bedding they could find. There were velvets and terry cloths, batiks and patchworks, paisleys and polka dots and shawls with knotted fringe. When they were done, they sat in the middle and ate pink cake.

"You didn't eat a *W*," Frankie said. "You ate a *B*."

Uncle Eric's eyes went big and bright. "No fooling you, Sister. What else do you know?"

Frankie licked icing from her fingertips. "I know my mother will never be the same. I know my father wants to run away. I know I'll lie to Father Greg." Frankie began to wrap a long scarf around her baby doll. She started with its feet and wound the scarf around its body until it was a tight, lavender cocoon. She handed it to Uncle Eric. "And I know I want Jasper to make it but he won't and that James will be the one who lives instead. And I already don't like James because he's the reason Jasper won't live."

Uncle Eric was as quiet as Frankie could imagine a person being. She looked at his long eyelashes, at the way his lips seemed stained with wine, his eyelids stained with ink. She watched his slender hands, how his fingernails were all different lengths, some as short as a construction worker's, some as long as Miss America's. She watched as he wrapped the baby doll in a second scarf. Then he handed it to Frankie and she wrapped it in a third. Then she handed it back to him for a fourth. They went on like this, silent, back and forth with the doll, until it was dark outside and the cicadas were as loud as a thousand wire brushes on drum skins and the baby doll was the size of a Virginia ham and they set it in the nest like an egg and went to bed in the guest room where there were still some blankets.

"So, you don't know Loretta?" Uncle Eric asked in the dark. Frankie shook her head on the pillow. "She was born in Butcher Hollow, Kentucky, and she had three sisters and four brothers and she got married when she was fifteen."

Frankie was thinking of her patent leather shoes. She was thinking of the box they came in. She kept seeing Jasper in the box. She kept trying, in her mind, to cover him up with tissue paper but the tissue paper kept sliding off.

"She's had sixteen number-one songs." Uncle Eric lit a cigarette as they lay in bed. It crackled red in the dark, then he exhaled. "'Somebody, somewhere don't know what he's missin' tonight,'" he began to sing, in a way that almost sounded like talking. "'Lord, here sits a woman, just lonesome enough to be right. For love 'em or leave 'em, how I need someone to hold tight.'"

In her mind, Frankie was able to pull the tissue paper completely over Jasper. But through it, she could still see his face. Like Uncle Eric's in the cellophane envelope.

Uncle Eric gave a little laugh from his side of the bed. "Oh, Sugar," he said. "I can't sing worth shit. But I sure have had a nice time with you."

Frankie pretended to be asleep. Downstairs, she could hear the click of Uncle Eric's stoplight as it cycled through its colors. She knew you couldn't hear that click in the real world. No one out there knew stoplights made any sound at all.

*

In the morning, Frankie woke to the sound of crying. It was Uncle Eric, back in his bedroom, sitting at the window with the last piece of cake, looking out at a gray windless day.

Frankie came and stood at his side. She could see the windsocks drooping from the trees like real socks. "Which one was it?" she asked.

Water ran from Uncle Eric's eyes. Not from one corner or another, but from the entire eye. "The little one," he whispered. "He never stood a chance."

Frankie thought of her ruined parents. She thought of James, at the age of nine, fat, in a baseball dugout. She thought of Uncle Eric's hip, how the bones were like two puzzle pieces that didn't fit, but how doctors had pushed on them anyway to make it look like they had finished something. And Frankie thought of her gray wool coat with the brass buttons. It had been hanging in the back of her bedroom closet since Thanksgiving, and in its inner silk pocket, still wrapped in one of Uncle Eric's napkins, was the quail—*her quail*—tucked into its nest.

SUNDAY

P AUL LEMMON DIDN'T like to talk about the way his son had died. Why any father would want to talk about how his kid had died was beyond Paul, but there were some who did. There were some fathers who had to talk about it over and over again, like they were hanging the memory on a clothesline and their yammering on and on was the sun, just bleaching the sadness out of it, fading the death into something they could handle wearing. One time, Paul had gone to a support group for grieving fathers, held in the basement of some cold, broke Baptist church, and the men launched into their various tragedies as if it made them feel better to do so. Paul had sat on his folding chair in that fluorescent circle and listened to the lurid details of two drownings, a stabbing, a choking, an accidental gunshot to the head, a car accident, three overdoses, and an electrocution involving a baby, a bathtub, a curling iron, and a house cat.

When they got around to Paul, for his time to share, he whispered void of color: "Fuck all y'all." Then he showed them his nubs, where his arms used to be, one of which was long enough to wear a pirate hook, which he could tell the men admired, and he said: "Let me tell you something no one knows. Not even my new wife. About these here arms, or lack thereof. Losing them wasn't no accident. I got rid a-them on purpose. Because after my son died, all my arms did was remind me I didn't have no son to hold no more."

The men looked at Paul like he'd told them he was Jesus and he was back and they were all in a shitload of trouble. Then he screeched up from the metal chair and left the meeting, but because he left early, Pauline wasn't there yet to pick him up, so when the rest of the men finally left the meeting and came out to the parking lot, Paul was still standing there, waiting for Pauline to drive up in the Corvette, and he had to interact with them. He had to listen to them say how sorry they were and he had to pretend like he was capable of accepting their horrible apologies. And he had to act like he was a decent person who wouldn't replay their children's deaths to make him get his mind off his own child's death.

*

Pauline could best tell the story of how Paul lost his arms. She could tell it as if she'd been there, to anyone and everyone, to those who looked at Paul's nubs out in public and those who had enough decency not to. She told it as a cautionary tale, as entertainment, as if it were no big deal, as if it were the only deal. She told it as if it were the first chapter of Genesis, the last chapter of Revelations. She told it in a way that Paul came to adore, because the way Pauline told the story made it all seem true. It made Paul seem like a victim. It made Paul hate himself just a little less. He could always see the story working its way up in Pauline, in a waiting room, in line at the grocery. She'd twist and turn and wring her hands until the story came out of her like a sneeze on the face of whoever would listen, whoever would pretend to.

"Oh, it was something else," she'd burst. "Two years back, when

Paul worked at Weiss Meat Processors right before we met, someone somewhere high up at the place decided to put in a new machine that cut baloney into shapes. It was for the kids, right, Paul? That's right. A promotional gimmick that cut the baloney into dinosaur shapes. Was that ever a mistake if I've ever heard of one. I mean, all children like their baloney. No one needs to go and make the baloney any different for a child to eat the baloney. You ever heard of a kid who won't eat a piece of baloney? A kid don't need a piece of baloney to be shaped like a bronnysaurus to make them like it. Was some of them bronnysaurus-shaped, Paul? I think they was. I don't know my dinosaurs from my dogs, but that don't matter. What matters is the fella who trained Paul on the machine, come to find out after all this happened, he had an addiction with marijuana. So, that was part of the problem. The other part was that Paul didn't normally work that shift, but they asked him to stay and do a double, so you see how all this adds up to the sort of settlement that'll get you a Corvette. But don't you just know it, Paul agrees to do a double because that's the sort of man he is, a good man, and there's this new gizmo and Lord if it don't take less than ten minutes to mistake his arms for two logs of lunch meat before you can say scat. Pow!" Pauline would illustrate, stomping one meaty leg wherever they happened to be. "A pterosaurus on the right arm, down to the bone. Then, bam!" she'd stomp with the other meaty leg to even things out. "A stegodactyl on the left arm, clean through. I tell you, clean through like an apple corer."

At that point, if the person was still listening and hadn't walked away to compose themselves or escape, Pauline would go on. If they had left, she'd go on anyway, just for Paul, like she was telling him her story and not his. "I mean, baloney ain't hard. It's soft. What nobody nowhere can figure out for the life of them is why them blades was so sharp. Ain't nothing to cut through baloney. All's you really need is a butter knife. So, no wonder Weiss had to take the blame for it. And boy should they ever had. We may have gotten us a sports car and a new memory-foam mattress out of it. Might one day take ourselves a cruise to Alaska, but you can't ever make up for a man losing his arms. Never can. Can't get them back now, can you, Paul?"

To which Paul would always nod and Pauline would coo over him like a mourning dove and Paul would bask for a moment in the false glow that he hadn't stuck his arms in the machine of his own will. Every time Pauline was finished telling the story, Paul was able to momentarily forgive himself. For his accident, for his son's accident. For his impatience with—for his downright resistance to—rehabilitation. For choosing Pauline and an outdated hook over advanced prosthetics. Sometimes the story made Paul feel so good, he would even ask Pauline to tell it to him alone, at night when he couldn't sleep. And she would because that was what Pauline was: a marathon mouth.

It was the reason Paul had married her. She'd been his nurse in the hospital. The first to wipe his ass after the accident. As she'd wiped him with toilet paper and then a moist wipe and then flushed the toilet and pulled his pants back up and snapped off the hospital gloves, she'd told Paul all about an eight-piece set of porcelain figurines she'd seen on TV. They were made in Germany. They were the cutest little singing children she ever had seen. They had hair like an angel's. They had cheeks like apples. And Paul, humiliated that he could no longer wipe his own ass, a consequence he had not considered before he'd placed his arms under the baloney cutters, was just so grateful for Pauline's inability to shut up that he fell in love. He knew Pauline was someone who'd never, ever let there be a moment of silence when the world would close in on him and he'd have to remember his son's death and how he'd caused it. He knew Pauline would yammer enough to keep the memory of the accident, of the barn and the beam, from coming back to him, not to mention how Denise—pretty Denise, his first wife and son's mother—had left him cold, right there at the gravesite, right after the preacher had closed his Bible and Paul had dropped a blue carnation on the cheap, pine coffin. With Pauline in his world, Paul's previous one stood less of a chance of returning to him in still and lonesome moments, because there wouldn't be any still and lonesome moments. So, after that first ass-wiping, Paul ordered the set of German figurines by having another nurse call and order them, and then he had them delivered to the hospital and put on Pauline's portion of the nurse's station, where she kept a bag of miniature Kit Kats and her *I'm Not Fat, I'm Full of Love* coffee cup. And when she came into Paul's room crying and asked him what had come over him, that's when he asked her to marry him. She cried and cried and smiled and smiled and said, "Why, Paul Lester Lemmon. It would be an honor."

*

They got married where Pauline wanted: at the Bavarian-style chapel in the Bavarian-style town of Copper Springs, West Virginia, where Pauline wanted to move into a colossal A-frame after Paul told her she'd never have to work a day again in her life (other than doing everything for him) because he'd been given nine million dollars from the Weiss Meat Processors and all nine of that was hers. Paul was happy to move to a town where no one knew him or had known Denise or had any clue about the fate of his son who he could no longer refer to by name. And he was happy to marry a wife who knew none of it either, a woman he could make up his untruthfulness to in gifts: a chandelier the size of a hay bale, a curio cabinet stacked with German curios, a walk-in closet full of velour pantsuits, window boxes full of plastic crimson geraniums, an amethyst cocktail ring, an oil painting of Elvis Presley for the entry hall, a jumbo-capacity washer she'd wanted her whole life, a seashell anklet in the Walmart checkout she'd wanted thirty seconds. Pauline asked and Paul complied. It was the least he could do. She wiped his ass at least once a day. Sometimes three if she made enchilada casserole.

"I'll buy you anything your heart desires," Paul promised, usually on the toilet, in his moments of helplessness. "You name it, Pauline. You got it."

And Pauline would pat his back and tell him she loved him and that he was a good, good man. Her hero, in fact. And all she really needed at this point was the final set of German choir boys and then she'd be complete. "Them," she said, and one Friday night added, lowering her voice: "and a son."

Paul nearly fell from the commode. "A what?"

"A son," Pauline repeated softly, but then her voice regained its volume and momentum. "I ain't told you this, Paul, but I was born without a uterus. Well, not exactly no uterus, but a uterus that wasn't connected to nothing. It just floats inside me like a jellyfish. Never did have a period or nothing, which some gals might consider a blessing, but for me it was just a reminder that I was a broken woman. Good for nothing. I wanted so much to care for someone. That's why I became a nurse and then why I'm here with you and, oh, Paul, I'm not getting any younger. I want a son. I want to adopt a son. Won't you let us get ourselves a boy who has no future? A boy who's been shuffled from foster home to foster home who ain't never known what it feels like to be loved or hugged or have a room of his own?"

Paul said nothing. He was waiting for Pauline to finish talking, which he knew could take days. He was also waiting for her to wipe him.

"I've already been doing the research. I got me a brochure from the Appalachian Boys' Home. It's twenty miles over in Flat Lick. And, oh all right, I'll be honest. Last weekend when I said I was going to the Walmart for potholders and I left you here, I went on over to Flat Lick and had a look at the boys. They're the saddest sight I ever have seen. I had myself a good long look at all the boys, and I didn't take you because I didn't want you to tell me no and also, without the arms and all, I was afraid they would think we was there to get ourselves a handyman and not a son, so I just went over there by my lonesome like I was some single mother, and I already got one picked out to take on a day outing and I think you'll like him. His name is Gordon and he's six-four and he has a lazy eye and he's seventeen, which means we'd only have him for a year and I picked him because only a terrible person would say no to a seventeen-year-old who's never had a family. Only a terrible person would say no to a woman who's never had a uterus and I know you ain't that sort of man, are you, Paul? You ain't a terrible man at all." She paused to sniffle, then finally reached for the toilet paper and rolled a wad of it around her hand in preparation to wipe before stalling out and starting up again. "You ever go to the pound and look at the old dogs? They don't never get picked. Don't nobody want them. It's always puppies and kittens, kittens and puppies. Ain't ever the old Great Danes. Never. They just gas 'em. That or let them die on the concrete in a puddle of their own pee."

If Paul had had hands, he would have put his face into them

at that point, but he did not, so he just let his head hang as he sat there on the toilet with his pants around his ankles and Pauline stood there with her fist wrapped in toilet paper. "I don't want a son," he finally said. "So, I am going to say no. I want you to hear me saying no."

Pauline went silent. She wiped Paul and flushed the toilet and brought his elastic pants up around his waist and then she did not speak. For six days she was silent. She cooked and cleaned and took Paul to the toilet and wiped him and helped him off of it, but she did not utter a word. Without Pauline's constant conversation, Paul deteriorated. He began having dreams. Dreams he couldn't run. Dreams he couldn't scream. Dreams he'd never lost his arms in the machine and his own fists punched him in the face for what he'd let happen, for who he'd become. Everything returned: his son, the beam, the blood. The cold, blank stare. Denise's scream. On the sixth day, on the toilet again, Paul broke down. He sobbed and sobbed. Pauline stood stoic until Paul finally said, "Please. Please talk to me, Pauline." And Pauline said nothing and Paul sobbed some more and they both stayed there in the bathroom for an hour until Paul, broken and breathless, finally gave in and said: "Fine. Okay. You can have a son."

At this, Pauline squealed. She hugged Paul and wiped him and started talking without end about all the things she'd buy for Gordon: A trash can with an NFL team logo on it, a bed shaped like a plastic race car, a ceiling fan that resembled a ship's propeller, some of those fleece blankets that looked like zebra fur, two bean-bags, a video game console, a vintage Mickey Mouse phone off eBay, and five camouflage snowsuits because if December was any indi-cation, it was going to be a long, snowy winter and he might want to get outside and go sledding. Oh, and two sleds. Pauline talked while she made dinner and talked while she fed Paul enchilada casserole from her artificial nails. She talked while she bathed him and talked while he tried to watch that show where men almost die catching tuna. She talked until Paul felt like himself again, the one he'd become when she first wiped him.

*

On the Sunday that Pauline was scheduled to drive to the Appalachian Boys' Home to spend a trial day with Gordon, she woke Paul at dawn and sat him at the kitchen table and got out a yellow pad of paper and wrote at the top: SON DAY SUNDAY. Paul couldn't watch, but it didn't matter, because Pauline read from the list over and over until Paul thought he might erupt, until Paul wanted to scream: "No. No son! We're not going through with it!" but couldn't for fear Pauline would go quiet again and the rest of his days would be spent replaying the beam and the blood and his dead, blank son while Pauline wiped his ass and gave him the permanent silent treatment.

"First, Walmart," Pauline said. "I'm stopping there to get Gordon a new basketball before we pick him up. I can't pick him up without a gift and I don't know any boy who wouldn't like his own new basketball, especially one who's six-four because I'm sure he's had to play his whole life whether he wanted to or not. And then after that, number two: we're taking him to the Red Lobster in Farina to eat lobster because I bet he ain't never had lobster and then after that, three, I found a pediatrician who agreed to open his office on a Sunday to give Gordon a physical and then, four, I thought we'd get the boy a dirt bike, which maybe we should just go on and put that back at number one, at Walmart before we even pick him up. Yes, cross that off and put it at one. One, basketball and bike. Now then, back to number five, Pastor Tom. Pastor Tom said we could bring Gordon by his house before supper to have him baptized in his hot tub and then for six, I figured we'd come on home, back here, and present Gordon with a gold cross necklace, also Walmart back at number one—ball, bike, cross—and then eat tacos and then all sit on the sectional under our zebra fleeces and watch something as a family. A family, Paul. We're going to be a family, so maybe *The Lion King*. I think that appeals to any age, if you ask me. What do you think about *The Lion King*? I think it's perfect, and then, by the time it's time for bed, we'll drive him back to the boys' home and let him make up his mind, which he already will have and he'll beg to stay with us."

Paul said nothing. He began to relax. Surely, by the end of Pauline's harebrained day, the boy would be scared off for good. There'd be no chance of a second outing, much less a second son for Paul. Paul exhaled. He let Pauline feed him his scrambled eggs and dress him in his suit and polish his hook. He let Pauline help him to the backseat of the Corvette, where she covered him with one of the zebra fleece blankets so the owner of the Appalachian Boys' Home wouldn't see him.

"Not that it matters none," said Pauline. "I think they'd let us end up having him whether or not you was in the picture. I could tell they was impressed by the Corvette and my ring. But whatever the case, they don't know about you and I don't want to mess this up, so let's just let them think I'm the single mother that I say I am, and then when Gordon comes out to the car and we're about a mile away, you can pull back the blanket and sit up and say, 'Sorry if I startled you and all, but my name's Paul and if you like me I can be your father.'"

Paul, in the fetal position of the car he'd bought but couldn't drive, imagined how that would go over. If Gordon didn't strangle him or throw himself from the moving vehicle, he imagined they might be able to make it to the Red Lobster where he and Pauline would sit across from Gordon, trying to read his lazy eye, trying to determine if he was looking at them or not.

You like Alfredo? Paul imagined Pauline asking at the Red Lobster, just so she could prove she knew what Alfredo was, just so she'd have something to teach the boy, an opportunity to do something motherly. *Alfredo is a word for expensive, Gordon. But don't you worry about price. Your father here, see how he's missing his arms? You best be grateful for that. His arms, or his not-arms, have paid for my car and our house and your college education, that is if you end up wanting to be our son and if you end up wanting go to college, which I personally recommend, mostly so we can brag on you and say we have a son in college. But don't you worry about money, Gordy. If you want the Alfredo, you get the Alfredo, though I think you ought to get the lobster because today is a very special day and lobster is what you eat on very special days.*

Gordon would be shy and unconvinced but hungry, just like the Great Dane Pauline had once described, dead in its own pee. Paul imagined the stack of plates Pauline would marvel over. Two lobsters and Alfredo and fried shrimp, twenty pieces, and clam chowder and six Cokes and a side salad and two baskets of cheddar biscuits. The boy would be ravenous, partly because he was still growing and partly because he'd spent his whole life eating horrible food, but mostly because he was bottomless from not being loved. He'd have a hole inside him that could never be filled. Paul could understand this.

Pauline navigated the winding West Virginia roads, roads that Paul knew were dull and salted under a white December sky even though he couldn't see out the window. He allowed himself to feel a little pity for the boy. The boy had a hard day ahead of him.

If they made it to the pediatrician, which they likely wouldn't, the boy would sit on the child-size exam table and let the doctor look into his ears and eyes and throat. He would have to endure having his broken heart listened to, his abdomen prodded. Paul saw the doctor frowning at the lazy eye and providing an eye patch and the three of them leaving the doctor's office with the boy looking like a buccaneer.

If they were lucky enough to make it to Pastor Tom's after that, the boy would have to duck to enter the tiny ranch house. Pauline would no doubt bring out the Hawaiian bathing trunks from Walmart and tell the boy he needed to put them on and get in the churning hot tub on the crumbling deck and give his life over to Christ. Paul imagined there might be some resistance to that. They would leave with the boy furious and unbaptized, and Pauline, unwilling to admit defeat, would babble on and on in the car about the things she babbled on and on about: that God would always be ready for Gordon whenever Gordon decided he was ready, what Gordon might want on his tacos, a roadside deer here, a roadside deer there, an early blooming forsythia, an icicle that resembled Priscilla Presley, a sign for the World's Largest Teapot, her family members and what ailed them—Grandpa Turner: emphysema; Cousin Kevin: diabetes; Aunt Polly: shingles.

The boy would demand that Pauline pull the car over. He would throw open the door, leap out and scream from the gravel shoulder: *Fuck you! Fuck both of you! I hate you! I hate you! This has been the worst day of my life! Why would I ever want to live with people like you?* And Paul would waddle his body out of the car's backseat and gently confront the boy while Pauline fought back tears. Paul would calmly explain that Pauline meant well but was sometimes overbearing. And that he, Paul, understood disappointment. He'd tell the boy that he knew how awful life could be. He'd say all the boy needed to do was to head back to their place for a few minutes and take a glimpse at the room Pauline had fixed up for him and scarf down a few tacos and then he was a free man. No strings attached. A day he could write off as a weird experiment. Paul would talk the boy down, and they'd drive back to the house and Pauline would talk much less on the way home, scared of what her big mouth had gone and done, and they'd have a couple of laughs and Gordon would be polite enough to take a look at the room, and, while Pauline grated the taco cheese and *The Lion King* waited on pause, Paul would take the opportunity to talk to Gordon alone. To ask him what he liked and what he wanted to be when he grew up, which was just a year away. And Paul saw himself looking up at the boy and listening, but not really. He saw himself overjoyed, overcome, over the moon, not hearing a word. As Gordon talked, the world would go silent for Paul. Silent in a way that he could finally handle. And there in the backseat of the car, as the Corvette wound through the cold mountains, Paul began to love the boy before he'd even seen him.

BIG BAD

THE FIRST TIME Helen gave birth to herself, she was fifteen and a half. She drove herself to the hospital in her brother's Trans Am (she'd just gotten her learner's permit the Wednesday before), and by the time she squealed into the parking lot, panting and panicked, her red hooded sweatshirt drenched, a foot had emerged between her legs. To her amazement, the foot was her own, just an older version of the one crammed against the Trans Am's brake pedal, but this foot, the one kicking out one side of her soccer shorts, had a tendon-y elegance to it, not to mention chic red toenails instead of cheap, iridescent pink ones. Helen stared for a good half minute at the twitching extremity, at its slippery sheen and eager arching, until a contraction hit. Then she fell forward on the steering wheel and blared the car horn with her forehead. Soon enough, a nurse appeared with a wheelchair and brought her inside to an unamused doctor.

"Well, whadda you know," he said. "Looks like someone got herself pregnant."

At this, the nurse rolled her eyes. Helen frowned and unfrowned. She had a flash of time between contractions to consider the possibility that the doctor was right. That it was she, her own bad self, and not Dustin Mulhouse, who had knocked her up. She ran the day ("Boom-Boom Wednesday" was what they'd named it) through her mind. The sunlight had come down through the birch trees in Collier's Glen as if God was granting his blessing. There'd been a bottle of Rumple Minze. A little portable CD player playing Van Morrison. A plaid blanket that smelled of Drakkar Noir. The way Dustin had said *please-please-please* and she'd said *yes-yes-yes* was like something lifted from a romance novel. *Nope,* Helen thought. *That was no solo performance.*

"No one gets themselves pregnant," the nurse huffed, releasing the wheelchair brake with an angry kick. "Women aren't parthenogenetic."

Helen gave a little giggle. The nurse patted her back in a brief moment of sisterhood, and that was that. Helen remembered nothing from there on out. She did not remember the doctor lecturing her at ten centimeters about the reservoir tip of condoms and boys' one-track minds and how tarnished reputations never regain their sterling status. She did not remember screaming, the blood vessels bursting in her eyes, the twenty-nine-year-old version of herself being pulled out (beautiful, ballerina feet first) by four nurses and two doctors. She did not recall dying in labor, rising above the scene, seeing her parents and brother and Dustin weep and gnash and teddy-bear-and-tulip the room. She just went away, up to a little cumulonimbus, and let what was left of herself carry on.

Her new self wasn't all bad. But she certainly wasn't good. She was too thin and too willing and too quiet. She had already abandoned the notion of her own satisfaction (and her degree in biology) in exchange for perfection. Helen 29 was all about a man, Bill 54, who needed her to perform certain things to make him feel important and safe, most notably, smiling in approval and nodding in accord and tucking her bony hand into the crook of his camel-haired elbow at parties that celebrated nothing. Sometimes he needed her to arch her back this way, or kneel and pout that way, or to look at him from across a dimmed bedroom in a manner that erased who she really was for who he wanted her to be. These things made Bill feel palpably good, and Helen supposed it was only proper to share in his joy by acknowledging she had provided it. *It's like a meal,* she told herself. *You have cooked it and served it and now you must enjoy watching him devour it.* So she did. Helen 29 gave Bill the things he wanted: warm laughter and Christmas cards, an opinionated son, a compliant daughter, while he gave her bracelets and warnings.

As time went on, Bill wanted a third child: a roguish second son who would handle the sales and marketing of his life. He could see the son now. He could taste what the boy would do for him. *He will be my crown jewel,* Bill said. *The last act.* But Helen had begun to feel the wind through her body; she knew it was only a matter of time before she completely vanished. So, when Bill pressed her against the bedroom wall and entered her, when he held her hands above her head and handcuffed her wrists with his fat fingers, she let the seed take root, knowing full well there would be no second son, but instead a third version of herself. One so ugly that she'd be abandoned for a new 29, maybe a 24.

And that was how it went. Nine months later, when Helen's water broke in the kitchen, she sent the children promptly to the neighbor's, went upstairs and put on her pearl choker and pearl earrings and French perfume, then called for Bill to meet her at the hospital. Within an hour, Helen 29 was dead. The long-anticipated, russet-headed son with a knack for sealing the deal had not emerged as a consolation prize. Nor had a second, agreeable daughter. Instead, a third version of Helen, a forty-something, jowly wench with rolled-up sleeves and a curled-up lip arose from the puddle on the delivery room floor, marched over to Bill, and slapped two caps off his ivory smile.

Back at home, Helen was barely recognizable to her children. Gone was the lean woman with the weak half smile who acquiesced and habitually shrugged. In her place was a woman who meant business. A woman who'd had enough, except to drink. A woman who kept a coffee mug of Cabernet behind the toaster and couldn't be bothered by lipstick and knock-knock jokes; this new Helen needed comfortable shoes and chutzpah and charts taped to the fridge. There was no time for self-pity or vanity. There was too much to do. Casseroles and committees, appointments and disappointments, but above all else: *divorce.* Helen 45 had no time for anything other than everything that *had to be done.* Services for this person over here and that person over there, and things to mail and repair and wash and return.

Helen 45, fueled by thick coffee and sacrificial drive, never stopped to consider who she had become, until one day, at a shopping mall, a woman at a kiosk pulled Helen over to a mirror. She pressed both of her hands to Helen's cheeks and pushed her face up to the glass. "I am guessing," the woman said, "that you do not recognize this person." Helen was furious, but she could only look at who-she-now-was for so long before the anger turned to grief. Right there in the mall, an inch from the reflection of her limp hair and plain face, Helen began to weep. "I'll give you this cream," the woman said. "Rub it all over and you will be like you once were."

Helen complied. She bought the cream and she drank her wine and she told her friends what the woman had said. Helen's friends agreed. They went out and bought Helen things to wear that Helen had never worn before. Things that laced and snapped and lifted.

Things that suggested she could still provide the pleasure she had under the birches, the power she had signed over on the cul-de-sac. Helen's friends dressed her like their empty lives depended on it. They poured champagne down her throat. They reminded her of all the things she did for everyone other than herself, then they took her across town and propped her in a bar, a saloon really, and told her to do something for herself for once. Helen didn't know what this meant. Did it mean quilting? Container gardening? Giving this stranger here or that one over there, the one with the melting daiquiri, some portion of her flesh to knead or need? Did it actually mean doing something for someone else? The more she drank, Helen began to think this was the case. So, she moved six barstools down and threw four shots back and, forty minutes later, ended up giving a man with sad eyes and soft shoes twenty minutes of her time in a Microtel. This transaction required Helen not to exchange pleasure or power, but to deal in the currency of purpose.

"Tell me I mean something," the man said.

From beneath him, Helen whispered. "You mean something."

"Say it again," the man said.

But Helen would not. With each empty thrust, she could feel something inside her womb already growing. By the time the man lit a cigarette and called her a cab, the dot of an "i" had turned into a peppercorn. The next morning it was a raspberry. Helen could feel it clinging to her insides like a burr to a sock. She sensed the fourth version of herself would not put up with the things this version had.

Helen's children and friends were mortified that she'd let herself get pregnant—at her advanced age and on a one-night stand, of all things. But Helen found something rebellious in it. Some sort of unexpected joy. She went out and bought gypsy dresses and drank herbal tea and burned incense in the house. She read books on palm reading and chakras. She sold all the jewelry Bill had given her and used it to buy a plot of land stitched with hackberry trees. "We'll build a cabin," she told the children, who were nearly grown now. "We'll buy goats." But the children wanted nothing to do with a log house or bearded animals or her—much less a bastard sibling—so Helen spent her days alone in rubber boots and a coat meant for a man, walking the fields she'd paid for in diamonds, learning how to smile like she had on that day under the birches.

Inside Helen, the fourth version of herself grew quickly at first, but then slowed toward the end. At eight months, her stomach was little more than the size of a small melon, the sort that might feed a single child. A midwife helped her birth herself at home, in a tub filled with hot water and parsley, and after two pushes that felt more like sneezes, Helen 79 emerged small and bony, but strong and hale, covered in rumpled skin as smooth as suede. Her hair was as white and wiry as a horse's tail. Her eyes were both kind and mean. And once Helen 45 saw Helen 79, she approved and moved on, dying right there in the tub with a final relieved exhalation.

Helen 79 and the midwife buried Helen 45 in the backyard. They marked the grave with a coffee cup filled with wine and daisies. They talked about martyrdom and devotion, the male ego and face cream. Then Helen 79 paid the midwife in tarot cards before hitching a ride to her hackberry woods where, for twelve years, she lived alone and happy in a silver trailer with seersucker curtains.

Helen 79 let herself do as she pleased. She let thrift-store dishes pile in the small sink. She let her snowy hair grow to the backs of her knees. She let herself make things that made no sense: leaves glued to rocks, twigs stuck into the ground in serpentine shapes, moss tucked into her pillowcase where she could hear it grow. She ate dandelion greens and wild onions and fiddlehead ferns. She sometimes wandered into town with chartreuse-stained teeth and bought oatmeal and salt and cigars and tabloids and scotch. She smiled at people and they stared back. Sometimes she saw her ex and his third 29. He looked through her the same way the wind had once moved through her. Sometimes, she invited her children to visit. They would stand in her trailer, appalled. Her son would encourage her to sell the land for condominiums. Her daughter would wash and stack the cheap dishes, crying the whole time. On her children's final visit, they took Helen 79 to a doctor who asked her to do arithmetic, to say the alphabet backwards, to name silly things, like the capital of Finland and which actress starred in *Casablanca* and what animal veal came from. In the end, the doctor determined Helen 79 wasn't senile, just weird, and as a thank-you Helen kissed him on the mouth, long and hard, while her children buried their faces in their hands.

A day eventually came when Helen 79 knew the end was near. Her heart hurt, then it didn't. It hurt, then it didn't. Her heartbeat became one of pain, not-pain, and she began to prepare her goodbye. She gathered her belongings in little piles. Two for her children, four for her friends. An anklet here, a poem there, some dried apricots, a little dropper bottle of her old tears, a rose peeled like an artichoke, an old goat's tooth, and one emerald the size of a testicle they could all stab each other over.

In this process, Helen came across an old jar. It was the one she'd bought at the shopping mall. Inside, she found a mound of yellowed cream, which she dabbed under her eyes and across her cheekbones. As she did this, she could hear the woman say, "You will be like you once were." Helen used it all, scraping it from the jar, over her wrinkled lips and loose neck, across her melting breasts and abdomen. Then she went out into the hackberry trees and clutched at her aching heart and waited to die. But the ache only moved from her heart to her chest. And from her chest to her abdomen. And lower still until Helen gasped and realized there might be a fifth version of herself.

"How old?" she asked the trees. "What for and why?"

The trees had nothing to say and Helen didn't either, and as she stood to hug a hackberry and give the only push she was capable of, her last self fell from her—an oily, blind, she-wolf puppy no larger than a moccasin. She collapsed next to it on the leaves and let it wind its way to the hem of her dress. She had no energy to stop it from writhing up her leg, over her wrinkled belly, and onto her dry breast. Helen yelped at the wolf's needle teeth. She saw Dustin, her two children, her brother, her parents. She felt Bill behind her, the sad-eyed man above her. Then she looked down and saw herself below.

Up in the sky, Helen 79 met up with Helens 15, 29, and 45. They all lined up, the four of them on the cumulonimbus like unstacked Russian dolls, and watched the wolf. The pup nursed from a hackberry knothole. She gnawed on what was left of Helen. She nosed Helen's bones into a pile. While the bones bleached like birch branches in the sun, the she-wolf grew, right before their eyes, as long and blue as a cold steel blade.

"This is the best me yet," Helen 15 said. "An honest-to-God wolf!"

Helen 29 snorted. "You can say that again. You were an awful version of me. So careless and loose."

Helen 45 butted in: "Oh, shut up, 29. You were the worst of all of us. A complete sellout."

"Takes one to know one," Helen 29 said.

Helen 29 and Helen 45 went at it right there on the cloud. 45 called 29 "plastic." 29 called 45 a "martyr." 45 yanked off 29's pearl choker. 29 mashed her hands against 45's jowls. Neither of them noticed that below, the she-wolf was now being chased through the hackberry woods. A pack of he-wolves was on her trail. They nipped at her heels. Their noses knew what she had to give, what they had to take. She thundered through the underbrush. She panted, panicked, as Helen 15 had in the hospital parking lot, but there was no escaping her fate. Soon enough, the he-wolves overcame her. In a flurry of fangs and fur, they each had their way with her—mounting her, pinning her, teeth on her scruff, one after another—until she collapsed, limp and alone on the forest floor.

Helen 15 saw this happen. Helen 79 felt it happen. But the two Helens in between sparred, oblivious and hateful. Helen 15 nodded at Helen 79, and Helen 79 nodded back. They knew the time had come to turn back time, to be born again by never being born at all. Helen 15 climbed onto Helen 29. She stood on her thin and brittle shoulders until Helen 29 had no choice but to succumb and climb back inside Helen 15, from where she had originated, until all that remained was one ballerina foot emerging.

Helen 45 watched in horror. "Oh, no," she said. "Not this."

But Helen 79 was already on her knees, small and spry, crawling under Helen 45 and up inside her before 45 could resist. "Looks like it," Helen 15 said.

Helen 15 and Helen 45, each with an older version of herself inside, stood and faced one another. Below, the she-wolf nursed her wounds and resigned herself to growing whatever sort of seed took. She could feel it inside her already, a thorn in her fur. It grew at a rapid pace. The two Helens could see the wolf's belly expand before their eyes.

"We can do this the hard way," Helen 15 said.

"Or the right way," Helen 45 sighed.

The two Helens stepped forward and embraced. They held each other as the she-wolf went into labor. It was the most difficult of all the labors. More than 15 birthing 29. More than 29 birthing 45. More than 45 birthing 79. More than 79 birthing the pup. The wolf howled and paced. She made a bed of leaves and circled through them in one direction and then another.

The Helens didn't dare look to see what might emerge, another wolf or another Helen. At last Helen 45 dropped to her knees and crawled inside Helen 15, and Helen 15 was all alone on the cloud, her three other selves stacked within her, unborn, once again. She watched as the dark slit beneath the she-wolf's tail gave way to dark blood. The she-wolf birthed neither wolf nor woman, but parts. Male parts that hung and swung. Organs that didn't invite or entice, but commanded, demanded.

"Thatta girl." Helen 15 nodded in approval. "Now you're thinking."

Then, like a thrown stone, Helen 15 plummeted back to earth. She fell right into Collier's Glen, past the sunlit birches and onto the plaid blanket. She looked and saw: there was the portable CD player. There was the Rumple Minze. There she was in her red hooded sweatshirt and soccer shorts. Inside her pocket, she felt the fresh plastic edge of her learner's permit. Helen cocked her head and listened. Far off, there was rustling. It was heading in her direction. It might be Dustin Mulhouse coming to take all she had to give. But Helen hoped it was the he-wolf, hunting her down. The sixth version of herself could shred her and all the Helens inside to bits. He could scatter everything they had once been all over the forest. Their pleasure and power and purpose, their pearls and emeralds, their dumb ideas and blind faith. Helen was nearly in ecstasy at the thought. She lay back and waited, breathless. She would be her own lover, her own killer. She would be her own man.

DRAWERS

HALFWAY BETWEEN CLIFTON and Merona, the sun breaks through the colorless sky like a circle of light in an operating room. It bleaches the empty highway, exposing Lawrence's car, which moves hot and solitary down the road, a loose ember blown. Here is where the gray lint of Spanish moss chokes the trees, where the soil fades from red to pink, where Lawrence knows he is most trapped, dead center, equally removed from his home and Susan's. Here is the merciless heat, the Florida farmland where livestock move as if in quicksand, as if already stew meat.

On the roadside, a fence is being built. The workers, oily with sweat, set posts with shovels and hands instead of machines. Lawrence imagines a posthole, a man stumbling into it, a femur snapped in two. He imagines a tumbleweed of barbed wire, palms lacerated, flies swarming. He imagines flies, their larvae, multiplying by the billions, teeming dunes of white rice.

As he imagines this, Lawrence recalls something from his childhood. How once his father, on a rare day he was not on call, took Lawrence quail hunting. It was after Lawrence's mother's death and neither had anything to say, so they walked the Georgia pinewoods in silence. They had no luck with quail, but they came across a wild pig, a dead one, sliced from throat to tail by a hunter's knife and left to rot. Its insides crawled with white worms so numerous and frothing that Lawrence thought at first the hog had been sprayed with a fire extinguisher or filled with shaving cream.

"Well," his father said plainly. "There's nature for you."

His father found a stick and opened up the pig, angering the worms, horrifying Lawrence. He named the organs he could name. *Liver, lung, pancreas.* Lawrence hugged a tree to stay standing, eventually bent over and was sick, and his father pretended to notice none of it. They returned to the pickup truck the long way, his father calmly pointing out lichens and songbirds on the walk back. His father took his time, as if purposely prolonging Lawrence's pain.

This, Lawrence had forgotten. And now, in remembering, he has lost track of where he is. His eyes have been in the old Georgia woods, on the pig, the worms, but here he is: back on the hot, white Florida highway. And there is the horse. Standing in the middle of the road, as if a movie backdrop has fallen, a looming, dun-colored roadblock coming up fast. For an instant, Lawrence thinks it must be a mirage, his imagination finally getting the best of him, and it's then he barrels into it—a warm boulder dropped from the heavens. The car lurches like a seesaw. Lawrence pitches into the steering wheel. He pitches back against the headrest and glimpses the horse's hide up close as it's vaulted over the hood and windshield, a sudden show of wiry mane and golden dust released. Then there is a sound Lawrence knows he will never forget. A groan both mechanical and animal. It radiates to his core, as if his spine is a metal string, plucked by fate's unforgiving finger.

*

Lawrence's daughter, Susan, calls to let him know she is having a party. The baby will be circumcised and his presence is requested.

"Don't bring a gift. Just yourself," she says. "That is, if you're up to traveling. Are you getting out much?"

"In public?" he asks.

"Yes," she says. "Are you at least going to church?"

"Not *me* public," he clarifies. "The baby public. He'll have this done to him in front of people?"

"Well," his daughter says with a laugh that's both diffusive and defensive. "In our living room. However public you consider that."

Lawrence doesn't respond. He knows his silence is mistaken for an opinion on Susan's new faith, but imagining the scalpel, the penis, he is speechless. Where will the foreskin go, Lawrence wonders? Will it be displayed on a sterling saucer for the guests to admire? Will it be sealed in a baggie and thrown into the kitchen garbage like a vegetable paring? Will there be a place where Lawrence can go lie down if he needs to go lie down? Moreover: Will Susan's new family serve food that too closely resembles the animal it came from? What, he frets, do Jews eat at circumcisions? Will there be a fish with its head still on? A large salmon with a milky eye? A cod whose exposed gills still gape from suffocation? It occurs to Lawrence that there may be a dish of nuts, unshelled macadamias perhaps, alongside an heirloom nutcracker. If this is the case, Lawrence feels certain he will imagine the nutcracker clamped around an actual testicle, while the in-laws ask him how his hollyhocks are.

"Still growing hollyhocks, Larry?" one of them will ask.

"Yes," Lawrence will whisper, as the testicle bursts in his mind. And then he'll collapse on the floor as if kicked in the groin by a steer, the crowd falling silent save for the whimpering of the freshly circumcised baby, and Susan will come to his side with a glass of tap water and rub his back and the whole ruined day, much to everyone's silent dismay, will once again end up being about him: Lawrence Fields, the recently widowed widower who's been having a hard time getting his wheels back in the ruts.

These are the things that have haunted Lawrence since Anne's death: the ugly truths, the fish heads and foreskins. He no longer goes to the post office and sees boxes and envelopes and imagines love notes and hand-knit sweaters. Instead, he sees divorce papers, sperm samples, chunks of heroin, hate mail. When he goes to the grocery, he does not see a pound of hamburger meat; he sees an Angus, electrocuted, its throat slit, its knees buckling, its hooves chopped off and saved for school glue, its body pushed through a sieve. When he goes to the movies alone and sees couples holding hands, nuzzling over popcorn, he does not imagine them going home after the credits roll to have the sort of relations he and Anne saw fit to have, the sort where a man and a woman lay like flatware in a starched bed, a nightgown lifted at the back, a fly open for the time it takes, a gasp as if they've both spotted a rare bird, an offered tissue, twin goodnights. On the contrary: he sees two figures, tangled as if thrown from a height, faces thrown back in agony, skin clawed and mashed and kneaded in desperation, as though the man and woman are climbing out of hell on one another's bodies.

But to answer Susan's question: Lawrence is not, at least, going to church. The last time he was there was for Anne's service, at which he sat in the front row, dabbing a handkerchief about his forehead as he pictured his wife soon underground, the weight of six cubic feet of fresh earth straining the coffin hinges, pushing the quilted silk an inch from her nose. Lawrence had pitched forward in the pew, white and breathless, and Susan had done her best to fan away his terror with a funeral program while the congregation murmured and the minister paused and the organ's last notes hung in the air like a distant siren, but it had a been a futile effort on her part. So, no: he has not been back since.

*

The drive from Lawrence's house in Clifton to Susan's house in Merona is just under four hours. Lawrence figures he can do the drive without using a public bathroom if he forgoes his morning coffee and relieves himself in his own bathroom right before leaving and in Susan's powder room immediately upon arriving. But at seventy, his bladder has been known to betray him, so there is no guarantee this will be the case. Lawrence wavers, pacing, eventually honest: he must prepare something to urinate in. He goes to the kitchen and soaks the label from a mayonnaise jar, then he dries the jar and sets it on the counter only to imagine it rolling about the car, its visible golden contents sloshing, a specimen of lukewarm humiliation. He decides that something opaque might be better, maybe the plaid thermos he once used for lunch soup. He knows this is appalling, but he will not, cannot, venture into a gas station men's room.

Without Anne, Lawrence is back to who he was before: the boy who watched girls at ballroom dance class and thought only of his father's medical book, the pink reproductive system shaped like a sheep's head. He's once again the boy who slouched on the sidelines at football games and heard the fabricated crack of spinal cords, the one who imagined school buses plunging over overpasses, classmates exploding from them like sparks from a firework. He's the boy who once went into a men's bathroom and, upon seeing a pile of human feces in the urinal, ruminated for two months on how that scenario came to pass.

Without Anne, Lawrence is back to when it all began: age eleven, his mother's funeral. During the service, Lawrence stared at the cathedral crucifix, at Christ's billowed ribcage and trussed arms and wondered, for the first time, horrified and faint: *How did the nails hold the weight of his body? How was Jesus nothing more than a wet towel hung up by thumbtacks?* Lawrence heard nothing of his mother's contributions to the Women's Club or of her devotion to the good cause of literacy or of her notable knack with camellias. He thought little of how his life would change without her, of how it would now be him and his father and tough steak and canned potatoes and goodnights with a distant, unperfumed silhouette in the bedroom doorway. All he saw that day were Christ's shoulders dislocating and the nails tearing through his palms and the Son of God dangling like a child's loose tooth.

Anne had saved Lawrence from religion's gore. He followed her to Walnut Ridge Church, where the communion wafers were wheat not bonemeal, where the wine was wholesale red table not blood. There was no talk of stigmata or abortion. No statues of weeping saints. No cardboard rice bowls printed with pictures of starving children. Above the altar hung no crucifix, just a maple, lowercase *t*, that conjured, for Lawrence, feelings of clarity, charity, country lanes and roasted chicken. The homily, the whole experience really, was cerebral; there was nothing ghastly or corporeal about any of it. Every Sunday, when the service was over, the congregants gathered for black coffee in the vestry where they talked of the relative humidity, of zoning laws. Then, after just enough socializing to make them feel human but not trespassed against, Lawrence and Anne would return home, feeling nothing near guilt, but something near hunger, and before they ate their egg salad sandwiches on the porch by the hummingbird feeder, they said grace silently and separately without fanfare or fuss.

Lawrence places the washed mayonnaise jar in the cabinet and decides. Plaid thermos it will be.

*

When Lawrence raises his head, he sees glass on the passenger seat, a fly already on the dashboard, opportunistic. The car releases a resigned hiss out into the still day. Lawrence looks for the rear-view mirror, but it is gone. He touches his nose and there, on his fingertips, is the beginning of blood. He turns to look out the back window, and he can see the horse, an unmoving mound in the road. Lawrence stares at the highway behind him for oncoming cars. In the far distance stands a fence worker, a black post on the horizon.

Lawrence tries the front doors, but they will not open. He works hard to pry his knees from under the steering wheel, rotating his old body toward the backseat. As he frees himself, Lawrence feels he is crawling toward some elusive surface, like an animal in tar. He pauses, panting, on all fours on the front bench seat, before continuing, limb over limb, into the back, where he gives out, on top of his suitcase, a carcass washed ashore.

His suitcase is packed the way his father taught him to pack: in neat, necessary squares of shirts and briefs, handkerchiefs and pajamas. He thinks of this as he tries not to think of the horse, up and over the car. Again and again. The horse up and over the car. Three mammoth thumps. The first, on the windshield, the loudest. The second, on the rear of the car, invisible. The third, behind him, the end. The groan of pain and metal. Lawrence presses himself against the suitcase as the horse rewinds and replays. Up and over the car, squares of shirts and briefs. Up and over the car, handkerchiefs stacked like white envelopes.

After his mother's funeral, Lawrence and his father had gone home alone. His father did not turn on a single light in the house, and in the silent dusk they went from room to room, drawer to drawer, shelf to shelf, still dressed in their black suits, and put like things with like things. Yellow pencils bound with rubber bands like firewood, bars of soap stacked like marble slabs, soup cans lined like steel barrels. "Order," his father said, as they worked, "is all we have now, Lawrence." When they were done, his father went and lay down on top of his made bed, still wearing his shined oxfords, and Lawrence went upstairs to his room alone and opened his top bureau drawer. In the night, by touch, he rolled his white socks into unhatched eggs, then lined them up, all in a row, some light in the dark.

Lawrence, at last, rises on the backseat. He wipes his forehead. He collects his green banana, his thermos, his small suitcase. He tries a rear door and opens it. He climbs out into the heat. He can feel death, like a low voice calling to him, before he even sees the horse.

*

Lawrence stands in his kitchen, unsure. If Anne were here, she would get the small red cooler from its place in the basement and pack it with egg salad sandwiches wrapped in waxed paper and jumbo pickles rolled in aluminum foil. She'd line the cooler bottom with chilled bottles of water to keep things cold without smashing the bread. She would pack her purse with aspirin and antacids, a book of crosswords, bifocal clip-ons, moist towelettes. She would bring along two pillows because Susan's were always too soft, and two blankets because Susan's were always too thin, and a roll of toilet paper for her and a roll of toilet paper for Lawrence, because that was what decent people did.

But Lawrence ruins a dozen eggs in his attempts to boil them and peel them and make something resembling egg salad. He is out of waxed paper. He cannot find the moist towelettes. Bottled water will only increase the likelihood of thermos usage. Lawrence remembers what Susan said: *Don't bring a gift. Just yourself.* So he quits. He places the thermos on the counter for tomorrow's trip, alongside a single green banana and his car keys. The eggs smell strong in the kitchen garbage, so he takes the bag to the curb, to the metal trash can, then returns to the house and washes his hands. He does not look in the mirror at his long jowls and long nose and long ivory teeth, at his face that has not resisted but has just let life have its way. Instead, he puts on his pale blue pajamas and crawls into his cold side of the bed.

In the dark, he stares up at the green light of the smoke detector. He imagines a house fire, burned flesh, a victim's shiny, noseless face with two black holes for breathing. He imagines raccoons at the trash can, chittering and smart, peeling the eggs like he was unable to peel the eggs. He sees them rifle through his junk mail, past the egg carton and down to a baggie holding a foreskin, which they remove with their tiny black gorilla thumbs and hold up to the moon before dropping it in the middle of the street.

Anne had been the picture of modesty and discretion. A woman who gave off no signs of impropriety, perspiration, menstruation. Lawrence had sensed this when he'd first seen her in the dentist's waiting room, her ankles crossed, her skirt pleated, her eyes focused on her word find. On their first date, she folded her napkin on her chair seat before going to freshen her lipstick. On their second date, at the end, she offered her powdered cheek to Lawrence. On their third date, Lawrence, bewildered and disordered by wanting more of Anne, was relieved by Anne's prudence. Back at her place, upright on her sofa, she placed his hands where they were to go and when. It was as ordered as a recipe, a math formula. When they were finished, she put Lawrence's hands back where they belonged with two concluding pats. This Anne did every time afterward, with the clinical precision of a surgeon. In this way, she ordered Lawrence's inner world, his latent, perplexing wants, just as his father had ordered his shelves. Anne showed Lawrence how to file lust next to pencils, how to stack his desire like soaps. For Lawrence, this compartmentalization was synonymous with love. He knew he could not live without her.

At some point, the green light of the smoke detector fades away, and Lawrence falls asleep. All night he is fitful, dreaming that he and Anne are horizontal on a sofa that isn't hers, making out like they never made out, his hand up her skirt like his hand had never been up her skirt, reaching into her, over and over and over again, in a way that is foreign, as if he is reaching behind the couch to retrieve a dropped peach, reaching behind the couch to retrieve a dropped peach, reaching behind the couch to retrieve a dropped peach. In the morning, he wakes exhausted. He hasn't slept at all. When he goes to rub his eyes, he thinks for a moment his hand smells of fruit.

*

The highway to Merona is empty and hot. The sky is the color of gauze. Alongside the pecan farms, there are no signs for pecans but there are signs for boiled peanuts and roasted peanuts and ones warning of Jesus' return. *He Is Risen*, they say. *He Lives*, they warn. *He Is Already Here.* Near the border, Lawrence passes more billboards he does not want to read but cannot resist reading: *No-Needle Vasectomy. Divorce $89.99. Orchid Spa: Truck Parking.*

"You know what those spas are, right, Lawrence?" a fellow CPA once said. "You go in for a massage and they give you five minutes of a back rub before they tell you to flip over. You don't even get a choice. You have to do it. Then they give you a hand job and you give them a Jackson."

Lawrence had pretended to already know this. He had pretended that it didn't bother him. He pretended, when he went home that night and watched Anne iron his shirts, that he wasn't imagining her naked while a masseuse stood behind her, her tongue at Anne's earlobe, her hands over Anne's breasts, her fingers spread apart just enough to show Anne's nipples. Instead, he took his ironed shirts and hung them in the closet the way they were meant to be hung. Blue shirts by blue shirts, white shirts by white.

When Lawrence learned of Anne's diagnosis, he'd gone home and made eggs of his socks. When she began her descent, he shined his shoes. When Anne was no longer herself, in those weeks of madness, when she turned ugly and crass and defiant, when she lost all control of her faculties, both physical and mental, and walked the house naked and relieved herself in the yard and called Lawrence names he did not know she knew, Lawrence spent his days putting things back in the drawers that Anne had dumped out. He put forks with forks. He filed his disgust next to despair. In the end, Susan came to help. She took Anne someplace else. To a place that knew what to do with her, where like went with like. Susan relieved him. And Lawrence had been relieved.

*

On the roadside, Lawrence stands for a brief moment as if waiting for a bus. In the heat, he removes his tie and drapes it over his forearm. He removes his coat and does the same. His nose is bleeding good now. He sees: the horse is enormous, a sand dune in the road, almost white in the sun. Lawrence must resist the urge to go to it, lay upon it, feel its coarse, rounded side beneath him. "Hey!" he hears the fence worker call, still from afar but closer now, waving his hat like a flag. "Hey, man!" Lawrence responds by regarding the horse a final time, then walking, then trotting, then running. In a few minutes, he figures he will hear a siren far behind him; the police will come to block the road, to inspect the car, to marvel at the horse. In a few minutes, he will throw his tie and jacket into a culvert, remove his shirt, his belt, his pants. He will find an exit. He will stagger down it in search of a gas station where he can use the bathroom and drink from the sink and throw his plaid thermos into a trash can. He will handle a public phone. He will call Susan to tell her he is running late.

When those things are taken care of, he'll stand in his briefs and undershirt and loafers, with his suitcase and green banana, and take it all in: the fast-food restaurants serving Angus pressed through sieves, the hotels where men and women crawl over one another's bodies as if climbing out of hell. He will allow himself to finally see Anne for who she is: buried and dead—a snake winding in one eye socket and out the other, her lower jaw falling from her face like soft fruit, her ruined brain now just a smear of paste. He will allow himself to see who he was before his mother died: a boy who could crack a live turtle with a hammer, who could tie a brick to a deaf kitten and drop it into the creek's dark bend, smiling. He will allow himself to take another look in his father's bottom drawer, the one Lawrence opened once and once only, the one with the lined bullets, and the stacked pistols, and the magazines of women sprawled and arched in utter disarray. He's the sort of man who might visit one of those roadside spas. He's the sort who might seek one out on purpose, not just on a whim. Lawrence continues on, hot and winded, and he knows, he sees, what will come to pass. He's running down a road. He's stumbling down an exit. He's going up to one of those spas and staggering toward its door to have a better look. If the door is glass, he'll cup his hands around his eyes and take a good look inside. But if the door is plain and windowless, he'll have no choice but to knock.

THE ENTERTAINER

MRS. BILLINGSLEY ASKS Rachel's mother, not Rachel, if Rachel would like to accompany them to the beach for two weeks. "There's no television, no AC. It's almost embarrassingly primitive, but Rachel is just so entertaining. Such a delight. I know she'd make my girls happy."

This is how Mrs. Billingsley puts it to Rachel's mother over the phone, one evening after Rachel has been particularly engaging at tennis, and Rachel's mother, in her outdated kitchen, still humiliated by her divorce, her hatchback, her teeth, replies: "Yes! Yes! Absolutely!" without even asking Rachel if going to the beach for two weeks with the Billingsleys is something she wants to do.

If Rachel's mother's own life is unsalvageable, her daughter still has a shot. She pictures what Rachel can look like in five years if she goes to the beach and puts on a good show for these folks, meets the people they know. If Rachel is willing to do her little song-and-dance thing at night while the Billingsleys drink gin, tell some of those Helen Keller jokes she picked up at summer camp while the Billingsleys scrape crab claws with silver forks, teach the talentless Billingsley girls how to macramé, lip-sync, hula hoop; Rachel, if she's lucky, might end up as decadently bored and unafraid as they are.

Of course, Rachel will have to learn how to starve herself, how to volley, how to operate aging dick, but these are small prices to pay. Rachel's mother can at least teach her something about the not-eating. *Think of your hunger as a wheelchair,* she'll tell Rachel before she leaves for the trip. *Something you can never get out of, but something that will get you where you want to go, even if it's uncomfortable.*

"I don't want to go," Rachel says, when she learns of the plans.

"Too late now," her mother answers.

Rachel feels like hired help, a jester for the elite. Rachel's mother feels something akin to hope, like the hand of God is touching her for the first time in a decade.

*

The Billingsleys fly to the beach in a private King Air twin-turboprop. The girls, Devlin, fifteen, and Davenport, seventeen, straddle Rachel agewise and know her only through the tennis clinic that Rachel's mother paid for, like her summer camp, on a low-interest Discover card. They buckle themselves loosely in adjacent leather seats across from Rachel and their mother and exhale in unison.

"Was there not a Lear?" Devlin says.

"Or a Citation?" Davenport adds. Their voices pout but their mouths do not, as if their faces are afflicted by a practiced palsy.

"The girls are used to jets," Mrs. Billingsley explains. "But this is what we get when the men have first dibs."

"Fuck men," Devlin says.

"No thanks," Davenport answers. "I'm going to be a lesbo."

Rachel stares at the sisters and they stare back in such a way and for such a time that Rachel begins to wonder if this is her cue to begin entertaining everyone. To start diffusing things, as she always does, with her nonthreatening plumpness, her simple face, her clever puns. It's why she was invited, after all: to do what she does at tennis. Introduce the joyless to the concept of joy—if not in a way they can experience, at least in a way they can witness.

"You know any lesbos?" Davenport asks. "You went to camp. Camps are crawling with lesbos."

Rachel waits for Mrs. Billingsley to chime in, to say something like, "Davenport, please," or "Knock it off, girls." But instead, Mrs. Billingsley tilts her head back for a nap even though the plane has yet to depart. "Lesbos," she snorts with her eyes closed. "What goes where?"

*

Rachel's mother works in the basement of a bank counting checks with the eraser end of a pencil. She hears three things, eight hours a day, five days a week: the *thipthipthip* of the erasers, the asylum hum of the fluorescents, the cheery, insufferable banter of her co-workers: all women, all obese, all over sixty. All of them inexplicably—infuriatingly—content with their lives.

"One of them told me a recipe for layered pudding today," Rachel's mother tells Rachel the night before her trip. "You should have heard her. You would have thought she was explaining how to deliver a baby. 'First there's a layer of vanilla pudding. Then there's a layer of strawberries. Then there's a layer of nondairy whipped topping.'" Rachel's mother groans. "It's called Cool Whip, you idiot. It doesn't make you sound smart to call it something else. It makes you sound like someone who's worked in the basement of a bank her whole, pathetic life who thinks calling Cool Whip nondairy whipped topping puts a stamp in her passport. Please. Like she even has a passport."

Rachel's mother looks hard at Rachel. "This is what it's come to,

Rachel. Pudding people. For a while there, your father and I had a chance to make something of ourselves. We were on the verge of a country club. But now? The city park."

Rachel remembers the first time she walked in on her father. He was standing in front of the bedroom mirror, using a can of hairspray for a microphone. "Who here's happily married?" he asked the mirror. "Can I get a show of hands?" Her father squinted his eyes, as if he were looking out past stage lights and into an audience. "What's that? Five? Six? Well, there you have it, people. Proof of aliens."

Rachel's mother puts both of her hands on Rachel's shoulders. "This is not a trip to the beach, Rachel. It's a trip to school. Study these people like you're going to be tested. Someday, you could spend a third of your year in a beach chair. You just have to work at it hard enough and then—abracadabra!—you won't have to work at all."

Rachel's mother smiles. She sees Rachel living like someone in a soap opera: lethargic with wealth. Her tan arm, now thin, stacked with bracelets to the elbow. A silver-haired man in linen shorts at her side. Rachel's mother sees Rachel with a husband so taken by her full lips and visible hipbones that he rewards her yearly with a new Lexus. Rachel, on the other hand, sees nothing but a container of Cool Whip. She's eating out of it with a ladle. Or rather: her hands.

*

In the air, somewhere between Delaware and the beach the sisters insist on calling "Ass Island," Davenport gestures loosely at the plane's amenities: a narrow drawer lined with packs of spearmint gum. A first aid cabinet equipped not for engine failure but hangovers, stocked with envelopes of Goody's Headache Powder. A breadbasket filled with boxes of animal crackers and buckled into a spare seat, like a neighbor's child the Billingsleys have agreed to transport but are set on ignoring.

"Animal crackers," scoffs Devlin. "You see any babies up here?"

"In your vagina," Davenport says.

Devlin and Davenport lean across the narrow aisle to punch one another in the upper arms for a time, back and forth like papier-mâché marionettes, until their arms are red and welted from shoulder to elbow. It's as if both have been grabbed and shaken by a middle-aged lover who's discovered he's been jilted for a pool boy.

"Trucey trucey?" Devlin asks.

"Vodka juicy," Davenport answers.

At this, the sisters set about making cocktails, and Rachel watches, spellbound. The girls are a study in contradiction, equal parts crude and classy, mundane and mesmerizing. Their hair is eternally slept on, piled on their heads like Caucasian turbans. Their silk dresses are shapeless but clingy, their expensive loafers intentionally mashed into slides. Their bodies, fed only candy, seem to consist of neither muscle nor fat. They can slump in the corner of a tennis court biting Skittles in half; they can scuff across a tarmac with unwieldy handbags concealing liquor; they can slouch in leather seats, knees agape to show a pearly slice of panties and still, somehow, exude regality. Their only accessible flaws, Devlin's fingernails and Davenport's bottom lip, both of which have been habitually and vigorously chewed, only serve, in Rachel's opinion, to humanize them, to mark them as either inwardly anxious or outwardly bored.

"Here," Devlin offers Rachel a drink. "It's a Stoli-and-Diet."

Rachel takes it and sniffs. Beside her, Mrs. Billingsley naps with her mouth open, gasping, as if she's slept alone for years.

"That," Devlin points at her mother, "is how you make a man fuck the nanny."

"No shit," Davenport says, tossing back the contents of her plastic tumbler and mixing another drink inside the bowels of her Italian purse. "And yet, they're still together. Because Daddy likes consistency."

"And Mommy likes money," adds Devlin.

For an instant, things go quiet. As if an intentional moment of silence has been observed for decency's death. Then Davenport belches, unblinking, and says to Rachel, "So, who did your dad leave your mom for? A babysitter? A secretary?"

"Don't say it's someone not young," says Devlin. "Because that is the burn of the century."

Rachel takes a taste of her drink. And then a second. She doesn't dare say why her parents split. That it was her mother who left her father. That it was her father who left banking for stand-up comedy, because he deserved—his word—*applause*. That her father now lives in a basement apartment with a recliner and a hot plate and an iguana he agreed to housesit but somehow got stuck with. That her father spends his days making long lists of catch phrases he believes will get him discovered, revered, iconized: *And that's the long and short of it, folks! Trust me, ladies and gents, I'm an expert! And that's what you call screwed, my friends!*

"He banged my French tutor," Rachel lies, having had neither French nor tutors. "She was twenty-three."

Devlin whistles and clucks her tongue in mock judgment. Davenport shrugs. "I've heard worse," she says. "At least he didn't bang you."

At that, Rachel finishes her drink. Davenport makes her another. Halfway through the third, despite her mother's warning, Rachel gets out of her figurative wheelchair and asks for the animal crackers. Devlin and Davenport watch unblinking as Rachel eats an entire box and then a second.

"Damn, bitch," Devlin says. "Save some for the Africans."

Davenport doesn't comment. She just stares at Rachel as Rachel eats, chews her lower lip as Rachel chews, and it occurs to Rachel, as the plane whirs on slow and rich, as the girls splay warm and drunk, that Davenport's lower lip and Devlin's fingernails are the way they are not because the girls are scared or bored, but because they're starving.

*

Ass Island turns out to be a private slice of Caribbean land, shaped like a hand giving the finger. Devlin and Davenport, immune to its grandeur and that of their beach house, give Rachel a passionless tour upon landing.

"This is our room," Davenport says. "We've got a view of the ocean, a view of the pool, a view of where Devlin screwed the gardener."

"How do you know where I screwed the gardener?" Devlin asks.

"Because I was watching," Davenport says.

Rachel sits on a bed while the sisters unpack by tipping their suitcases onto the floor of the closet. They each deposit a pile of silk dresses and sunglasses, bikinis and lighters, playing cards and menthol cigarettes, smashed shoes and loose Skittles. There's a pink plastic case that Rachel guesses might hold a diaphragm. A carved wooden box that must be for weed. When they're done, they take Rachel on a half-hearted tour of the shingled house and flowering grounds, pointing out useless things: not where Rachel can find an extra roll of toilet paper or a glass of water or a bottle of sunscreen, but where their father once had a seizure from too much cocaine, which window the islanders climb into when the Billingsleys aren't there.

"See these shotgun shells?" Davenport says, opening a drawer intended for silverware. "They come here and do drug deals. They use this house as a hideout."

"Just doing our part," Devlin says.

"Community service," Davenport agrees.

Rachel is too ravenous to be impressed; she cannot help but point to the refrigerator next. "Any diet soda in there?" she asks.

Davenport yanks it open to reveal a lone champagne cork and an old jar of cocktail sauce, then she turns, slow, and looks at Rachel. "Oh, shit," she says. "You're hungry again."

Devlin opens her mouth in awe, then closes it like a fish.

Rachel lifts her shoulders, then drops them.

Davenport thinks with the refrigerator open. "If we take you somewhere, will you eat for us?"

Devlin releases a gasp. "Oh, please," she whispers. "Pretty pretty?"

Rachel looks from one to the other. This is why she was invited, she sees. This is how to make them happy. "All right," she says, nodding her plain, round face. "I can do that."

*

At a restaurant meant for locals but appropriated by the sun-burned, Rachel sits while Devlin and Davenport order for her: a double-bacon cheeseburger, a bowl of conch chowder, a plate of coconut macaroons.

"Get her a beer," Devlin says. "Two."

"God, beer," Davenport says. "What I wouldn't."

Rachel watches them fight over the menu, as if they've never held one, as if it's pornography, a love letter, a treasure map. The waiter lets them keep it to peruse, which they do, producing a pack of menthols while they read it, smoking as if they've just had sex.

Rachel notices that the Caribbean sounds different from other oceans. It sounds like something Rachel knows, but cannot place.

"Jerk chicken," Davenport says.

"Fucking potatoes," Devlin adds.

When the food arrives, the sisters sit back and watch Rachel eat, their eyes glassy with booze and tears.

"Take it slow," Davenport says.

So, Rachel does. She eats the burger as if it's her first, the soup as if it's her last. She pinches up each cookie with her soft, ringless fingers and holds them up for the girls to see, sugar in the sunlight. By the time the meal is over, Rachel feels the feeling of a job well done—one hundred stacks of counted checks. A layered pudding, well-layered.

"Take a bow," Devlin says.

"No shit," Davenport adds.

Rachel does not refuse. She brushes the crumbs from her lap and stands. She bows stage left. She bows stage right. She bows right down the center.

*

That night at the house, from their twin bamboo beds, the girls show Rachel how they entertain themselves without television.

"Things to smoke," Devlin says, laying out cigarettes and joints like a picket fence on her bedspread.

"Things to drink," Davenport says, placing a bottle of vodka next to a bottle of rum on the nightstand.

"And things to play," Devlin says, thumping her skull as if she's thinking up something good.

"Like what?" Rachel asks.

Devlin runs an unlit joint under her nose and inhales.

"Sometimes Davenport and I pretend we're regular people. That we're not rich."

"Yeah," says Davenport. "We just lie here and say shit that rich people would never say."

Rachel frowns. "Such as?"

Devlin licks the joint and smooths it, like a child's cowlick. "Rachel can judge us," she says to Davenport. "Rachel can tell us if we sound poor."

"Oh, wow!" Davenport says, showing an emotion Rachel guessed her incapable of. An emotion Rachel feels compelled to nurture, to cup her hands around and blow on like an ember. "Would you?"

Rachel cannot imagine saying no. "Okay," she says. "For Skittles."

For a second, Davenport and Devlin further brighten, as if Rachel has offered to eat two slices of cake in front of them. "God, I love you," Devlin says.

Davenport says nothing, she just stares at Rachel until Rachel turns warm, and after an eternal minute, Devlin lights a joint and takes a long drag, thinking. "I'm gonna run to Sears," she finally says, releasing smoke. "And get me a new jog bra."

Davenport doles out two Skittles to Rachel. "Well?"

Rachel eats the candy. "That doesn't sound rich."

Davenport takes her turn. "I got summer teeth," she says. "Some are here. Some are there."

Davenport and Devlin burst into an unexpected laughter that sounds both magnificent and terrifying, the howl of two lean dogs. Rachel eats the rest of the Skittles off the bedspread while the sisters, beige and bony, pass the joint between them. Both of them could fit inside her body, she thinks. Davenport and Devlin could be dropped into her torso like two silk scarves into a basket. They could hide there, where the hunger lives, a little, shimmering, satin pool.

"What's your dad do?" Davenport asks out of nowhere.

"Great question," Devlin says.

Rachel has forgotten where she is, who she is supposed to be. "Oh," she says, coming to, declining the joint with a wave of her padded palm, imagining two scarves unfurling, down her throat. "He's an entertainer."

Davenport and Devlin look at each other quiet, then they clamp their hands over their mouths like they're at a funeral suppressing laughter. "Like an actor?" Devlin says.

"Like a rock star?" Davenport adds.

Rachel isn't sure what to say. "He just has this way," she says, "of putting on a show."

"Oh, our dad's like that, too," Devlin says. "He throws big parties and never shuts up. Sometimes he pays someone to play the piano."

Davenport wets her fingertips and pinches the hot end of the joint without reaction. "One time, he hired a magician for the coke-heads. You know. Cokeheads love card tricks."

Devlin nods. "And last Christmas he brought in an owl."

Davenport points at Devlin. "That's right. He found an owl under the house, down by the stilts, and brought it inside to show to everyone at the party."

Rachel stares. "An owl?"

"Yeah," Devlin says. "Did you know there were owls in the islands? I didn't. I thought owls were from a forest in Germany or some shit."

"Dad just walked in with that owl on a beach towel. Everybody went out of their fucking skulls and the owl didn't do a goddamn thing," Davenport says. "It had to be sick."

Devlin blinks slow, remembering. "It just sat on that towel and stared. Everyone was passing it around and Dad was standing there like it was no big thing except it turned out to be a big thing."

"A real owl," Rachel says.

"Turns out owls are beautiful," Davenport says. "Who knew?"

"Thanks, Dad," Devlin says, as if he's right in the room with them. "People were so-so before you brought the owl in, but now they're happy as hell."

Rachel feels something close to fear, rising. "What happened to the owl?"

Devlin lays down on her bed and closes her eyes. Davenport pulls off her shirt and sits there, topless, using her shirt to pat under her armpits. "It's hot," she says. "I'm wasted."

Davenport falls forward on her bed. Her tan, bare back is as slight as a child's. Rachel stands there, alone for a moment, thinking about the owl. She wonders if they let it go. If the owl let people touch it. She imagines the owl, startled, flying around the living room, the guests both delighted and afraid, Mr. Billingsley really getting his money's worth, even though it cost him nothing. Rachel leaves Devlin and Davenport the way they are: passed out, with the lights on.

*

In Rachel's room, Rachel finds Mrs. Billingsley on the bed, staring at the ceiling, a drink loose in her hand. Her stout arms are pink from sun. Her eyes are pink from gin. Her dress, also pink, is hiked up on one side to reveal a pale, dimpled leg.

"My girls," she slurs. "I do apologize."

Out the window, Rachel can hear the ocean but not see it. She still cannot place what it sounds like. "Oh, they're fine," she says. "They're fun."

"Pfft," Mrs. Billingsley says, shaking her head, jiggling a bit of her drink onto the floor. "Thank God they're rich. If they weren't rich, they'd be dead. They don't know how to do anything."

Rachel says nothing. She wants Mrs. Billingsley to leave. She wants to climb into the bed and think up catch phrases for her father. *What do I look like, an idiot?* She thinks of the one time she went to see her father perform. It had been late in the afternoon, in a bar that smelled of Pine-Sol. Only eight people had been in the audience and one of them kept saying: "Give it up, man. Give it up."

Mrs. Billingsley sits up on one elbow, takes a long swallow from her drink, the ice clattering back and forth like bracelets on an arm. "I wasn't born rich, Rachel. But I wasn't born poor either. I was somewhere in the middle. Like where you are. In that place where you don't know how good you got it." Mrs. Billingsley swings her legs over the side of the bed like she might stand, then she wavers and lies back down, gingerly, as if she's on a raft in water. "I was thirteen when I met Mr. Billingsley. I worked at the golf house on the ninth hole of the club we couldn't afford to join, and I served sandwiches to the men. Those were good days. Quiet ones. I worked with another girl. Her name was Beverly. We just listened to the whack of golf clubs. The hum of golf carts. We made lists of what we wanted in life. Cars and rings. Things, Rachel. Then we handed the men sandwiches. We didn't even have to make them. We just had to keep them cold. When I saw Mr. Billingsley, I told myself to do whatever it took to get him to marry me. So, I did whatever it took."

Rachel's hands are stained from the candy. She clasps them together as if in prayer and then unclasps them. Over and over she does this as Mrs. Billingsley talks.

"Oh, Rachel. I just did what it took. And look where it got me." Mrs. Billingsley reaches her arm down as if to put her glass on the floor, but the floor escapes her by a few inches, so she lets the drink hang in her swollen hand. "You'll meet him," she says. "He's old and angry and handsome and funny and everyone loves him, so I probably should, too. It's too late and too hard for it to be any other way anyway. Oh, God," Mrs. Billingsley sighs. "I'm so glad you're here, Rachel. You're such a delight. Can you teach my girls something normal? Something useful? Can you show them how to fry an egg? Can you show them how to fold a towel? Can you show them something, anything, they can use in life?"

Rachel thinks of the sisters, across from her at the table, waiting, watching, wanting. Their eyes are as pale as concrete, but whenever she brings the fork to her mouth, their pupils dilate with joy, like black ink dropped into water.

"Yes," Rachel says. "I can do that."

Outside, the ocean fades and crashes, fades and crashes. Finally, it occurs to Rachel that it sounds like applause.

DADDY-O

Daddy-o, the optimist, always came to town in his fringed vest and yellow van for the months that ended in *b-e-r*.

"I'm like a summer oyster," he'd say. "Can't nobody keep me down."

He'd show up behind the chain-link fence of W. G. Harding Middle School, a snagged autumn leaf clinging hopeful until Mabel looked his way, then he'd smile wide, teeth as white as bathroom tile against his Pensacola brown, and offer his daughter a little something for her time: a leather necklace greasy with patchouli, a temporary tattoo of a mermaid, a stolen red lipstick that insinuated Mabel was old enough to do what Janet Yuri did to Jimmy Overlay in the wide, shady mouth of the drainage pipe.

"Well, aren't you a bloomin' daisy?" he'd say. "Looks like I shoulda brung a stick instead. To keep the boys away."

And every fall, Mabel would play deaf to this and offer up a silent prayer of thanks that a palm reader in a low-cut blouse had seen divorce between Daddy-o's thumb and forefinger when Mabel was only nine.

✳

When Mabel moved seven miles over to Harrison High, she hoped Daddy-o would miss a beat. But on her first Monday of tenth grade at 3:30 sharp, she found him leaning against a bike rack with a dry hibiscus and a smile cracked white with remnants of Florida zinc.

"Guess who's coming to dinner?"

Mabel stared. Last time Daddy-o'd been in town, alongside a banded stack of his *Can Do!* pamphlets, she'd found a bowie knife in his glove compartment. She'd also found an old photograph of her mother graffitied with a felt-tip mustache. She hadn't been sure the duo was connected, but it did give her reason enough not to sit across from him in a restaurant.

"I already ate," Mabel finally said.

"Well, hot dog," Daddy-o beamed. "Let's go for dessert."

At the Dairy Queen, Mabel refused a soft serve cone. She knew letting Daddy-o treat her to something would make her feel beholden. She might even break down and confess that she sometimes imagined local meteorologist Brent Westerly as her new dad, the sort of man who would eat T-bones and make her mother forget how much she liked drinking. A man who would pay his taxes and own a set of encyclopedias and have his pilot's license. Mabel watched her father pay for a cone of his own by digging into a beaded satchel and producing a proud palmful of dimes.

"Milk does a body good," her father insisted. "You're missing out, Maybe Baby."

Mabel went to stand at the old jukebox where she watched the shaky metal arm reach out for 45s the same way her mother reached out for her after one too many wine coolers.

"Is he still so inexcusably *happy*? Is everything still so peachy-goddamn-keen for him?" her mother would slur. "Jesus. You'd never know he'd had the accident. You could bury the bastard in manure and he'd shovel his way out, grinning that crap-eating grin of his, looking for a unicorn."

"Bite?" Daddy-o asked, offering his cone.

"I don't think so." Mabel wrinkled her nose, then quoted her mother. "Not from a man who can't tell the difference between baby shit and butterscotch."

Daddy-o let loose with an amused hoot. "Now that ... ," he began.

"Oh, shut up." Mabel slumped down in the booth and watched her father's reflection in the stainless napkin dispenser. "Just shut up."

She waited for his face to fall, for Daddy-o's optimism to give way to defeat. But "Can Do!" was all he said, and he pulled an imaginary zipper across his mouth in the shape of a permanent smile.

*

During his annual backward migration from the Florida Panhandle to the Ohio Valley, Daddy-o's first choice in accommodations was the Happy Thicket Motor Lodge. He liked its brown canvas bedspreads, its tiny lobby that sold smoked almonds, its kitschy ice buckets painted to resemble little wood stumps. But he especially liked the motel's massive neon sign that rose fifty feet high from a cluster of tall white pines and blinked good tidings for all. It featured a glowing, spotted fawn that jumped a smiling log in three robotic flashes and a red, beaming *Happy* that made him just that.

"I tell you what'd be a laugh and a half, Maybe. Is if the owners of this here place had sense enough to screw a red bulb into Bambi there's nose come Yuletide." He squirted cheese from a can onto a Triscuit. "What all would that set them back? Ninety-nine cents and ten minutes on a cherry-picker?"

Mabel noticed her father's hand had assumed a quiver in the past eight months—a sporadic jerking not unlike the buzzing yellow

NO beside the sign's serene green VACANCY—and for a moment she felt compelled to entertain him. To tell him about biology class and how, last year, Peter Sawgrass had put the tiny snout of a dissected fetal pig inside his left nostril. Or how junior Dawn Beretti had lost the tip of her tongue at a slumber party when dared to lick peanut butter from a mousetrap. Or how, just today, she'd seen a bunch of pills in the girls' locker room toilet giving off strands of purple dye like Easter egg tablets.

"What do you think is more dramatic?" Janet Yuri had whispered to Mabel in English class. "Killing yourself or killing someone else?"

Mabel had shrugged, not out of ambivalence, but out of dumb wonder Janet would ask her opinion. She'd never worked a boy's button fly or known the bitter taste of sixteen aspirins on her tongue. She didn't staple her skirt hem three inches higher on the school bus or hide marijuana joints in her knee socks.

"I think both," Janet had mused. "A scorned lover and then yourself."

At the time, Mabel had silently agreed to disagree, but now, as she watched Daddy-o eating crackers through a smile, whose trembling hand remembered something he refused to, Mabel thought Janet was probably right. A person should have big reasons for dying. And unlike Daddy-o, big reasons for living.

Daddy-o squirted cheese on a cracker and held it out for Mabel. Two dots for eyes and a big cheesy smile. Mabel turned the cracker upside down so it looked like two eyes under a frowning forehead, then she threw it into the motel trash can. She no longer felt compelled to entertain him. He already was and for no good reason.

✳

"I find it works best like this," Daddy-o said on Wednesday. He stretched out as long as he could in the back of the yellow van, then folded his hands corpse-like across his chest and closed his eyes. "I start with my toenails."

Mabel stared up at the van's velveteen ceiling where Daddy-o had tacked a postcard of Tahiti, and a starry map of the universe, and a bumper sticker that said: *I Brake for Butterflies.* She wiggled her toes. Janet Yuri had passed her a note in English class with four scribbled ballpoint drawings and the words: *Pick One.*

"I think of coconuts and waterfalls," Daddy-o murmured. "I imagine a place where the lion lays down with the lamb."

Mabel had taken her time to decide. There'd been a stick figure hanging from a noose, a stick figure jumping off a skyscraper, a stick figure with red ballpoint ink spraying dramatically from its wrists, and finally, a stick figure lying next to a bottle of tiny black dots.

"Sleeping pills," Janet had whispered.

In the background, Daddy-o took a conscious inhalation. "'Hey, diddle, diddle, the cat and the fiddle.'" His exhale sounded like a long, exaggerated sigh of relief. "'The cow jumped over the moon.'"

Mabel had taken Janet's fate into her own hands. While the class read aloud from Shakespeare, she drew a fifth option: a stick figure being hit by an asteroid. *Ha!* Mabel had scrawled on the bottom after circling the scenario. *Ha! Ha! Ha!*

Janet hadn't seen the humor. For the remainder of English class she stared straight ahead, and when the bell finally rang, she dropped a note on Mabel's desk before storming into the hall.

It must be nice, it said, *to have so much to joke about.*

Mabel looked over at her father. There was that smile. That stubborn arc of idiocy. "Why did you draw a mustache on that picture of Mom?" Mabel asked suddenly. "Why do you keep a knife around?"

Daddy-o didn't open his eyes and he didn't stop smiling. "I thought if I made your mother look ugly I wouldn't miss her so much."

Mabel didn't buy it. "And the knife?"

This time Daddy-o opened his eyes and raised up on his elbow and his smile softened to a grin. "Remember this, Mabel. The happier you are, the more danger you're in. People fear goodness."

Mabel did buy this. She saw every day that misery loved company.

Daddy-o laid back down and closed his eyes and his smile returned less forcefully. "'The little dog laughed to see such sport,'" he whispered. "'And the dish ran away with the spoon.'"

*

When Daddy-o wasn't cleaning toilets for chump change, he was walking the streets with his seventy-five-cent *Can Do!* pamphlets, preaching and teaching to those willing to listen to his concocted brand of salvation. It was a little bit Norman Vincent Peale, a little bit John Lennon. It involved thinking positive and eight tracks of sitar music, incessant smiling and zoning out. Daddy-o called it a sunny outlook, an "attitude of gratitude." Her mother called it plain and simple denial. The proprietor of the Happy Thicket Motor Lodge called it nuts.

"That ole man a-yours," he said to Mabel in the parking lot. "He ain't right in the head. If I find drugs in his room, you can bet your ass I'll call the authorities."

Mabel stared. "Did you say something about my ass? 'Cause if you did, it'll be me on the phone."

"Well, well," the owner shook his head. "Someone sure don't take after her daddy."

"And it's not drugs," Mabel said. "It's optimism."

"I say it's drugs," said the man.

"I say drop dead," said Mabel.

＊

Janet Yuri cornered Mabel in the girl's bathroom at morning break on Thursday. "Well, if it isn't Little Miss Sunshine," Janet said. "Seen any asteroids lately?"

Mabel smiled, then fast decided against it. "I'm no sunshine."

Janet rolled her eyes. "Oh, sweetheart. You're as dark as a May day. I bet the worst thing to happen to you is a B. B-plus? Oh, sorry. A-minus."

Mabel thought of her father. How after the accident she and her mother had gone to visit him in the hospital. How her father had smiled through the bandages, how his swollen purple mouth could barely open for the straw that Mabel held to it. How he'd tried to whisper a knock-knock joke but didn't have the strength to get past the second *knock*.

"You know, Janet," Mabel heard herself say, "some people can't be broken."

Janet leaned in close to Mabel as if she might kiss her. "Oh yeah?" she said. "Like who?"

"My dad," Mabel said. "He's never down."

"Then he's a liar," Janet whispered, leaning in to unbutton the top button of Mabel's blouse. "Just like you."

＊

That day after school, Daddy-o drove Mabel out a winding country road to a fishing pond. He paid a man in a peeling shack four dollars, before backing the van right up to the water's edge and opening the rear doors so it looked like the two of them were floating at sea. Daddy-o sat on a tattered pink cushion in the back of the van and folded his legs underneath him and Mabel did the same.

"We're not fishing for fish today, Maybe Baby," Daddy smiled. "We're fishing for enlightenment."

"Hmph," Mabel said. "Looks like someone's out four bucks."

At that, Daddy-o laughed and laughed until his cheeks shone with tears. Mabel watched his joy with secret distrust and sad delight. The scar that ran along his jawline, as raised and shiny as a nightcrawler, was unaffected by Daddy-o's glee, unlike the three men who'd jumped him outside the bowling lanes, where he whistled while he worked as a janitor. They'd cracked him across the face with a baseball bat, because, as Mabel had heard her mother tell a neighbor: "He owed them thirty dollars for weed, but what they really wanted was to beat the smile off his face."

At last, Daddy-o stopped his cackling and grew as serious as he knew how. He closed his eyes and placed his hands, palms up, on his knees. "Some people say *om*," he said. "But I say *home*."

Mabel scowled. *Home* made her think of a scummy landlord, a parade of wine coolers on a Formica countertop, a stale plaid sleeping bag curled in a Volkswagen bus. Daddy-o read her mind.

"I don't mean *home* as in Apartment 7B, Maybe. I mean *h-o-m-e home* as in you and me both know we ain't from here." Daddy-o's eyes stayed closed as he said this, and Mabel watched him with fresh curiosity. He breathed in deep. He breathed out *home*. His face softened and thawed to something blank, relieved from the chore of constant optimism. When Mabel saw Daddy-o forget she was there, she closed her eyes and copied him, breathing *home-home-home* until she heard Daddy-o say, from somewhere distant but clear: "Let the things that get you down fall away."

The yellow van's dashboard appeared in Mabel's mind, and she imagined Daddy-o turning the steering wheel as far left as it could go. A line of his loose smoked almonds slid all the way to one end of the dashboard, then, one after another, the almonds fell to the floor until there were no more. Mabel followed suit, shedding herself of everything that got her down: the bowie knife, the beaded satchel of dimes, a noose, an asteroid, a handful of purple pills, her mother, and Janet Yuri. Her mother and Janet Yuri. Mabel, empty, felt herself rise. She felt herself breathe *home* until she was out, hovering above the pond, floating warm on her tattered pink cushion, a little levitating lily pad. Mabel looked down at the mercury thumbprint of water, out at the hills that blushed with fall. She could hear Daddy-o laughing, but she couldn't see him.

"Looks like I got my money's worth after all!" Daddy-o shouted.

Mabel looked left and right. "Where are you?" she called.

"Up here," Daddy-o called. "Above you!"

Mabel looked up to see Daddy-o twenty feet higher, flat on his stomach, swimming through the sky. "Looks like you got some work to do."

Mabel pushed down at her sides to move the air away, but only rose two inches vertically. "I can't go any higher!"

"We don't say *can't*, Mabel. We say *can*. That right there's your problem!"

Mabel opened her mouth to say *can*, but all that came out was: "Help!"

"*Can!*" answered Daddy-o.

"Help!" repeated Mabel.

Daddy-o swam down to Mabel with a grin. "*Can't* always seems easier at first, but in the long run, it's just more work." He lifted her cushion up over his head on one hand, as if to prove the ease of *can*.

"It's like I'm delivering a pizza!" Daddy-o cried, as they soared up to where the clouds looked like a dark afternoon rain. "A supreme one!"

Mabel caught herself smiling as they flew out over the countryside. Delivered was exactly how she felt.

*

That night, Daddy-o dropped Mabel off at home at eleven thirty.

"Christ, Wade." Mabel's mother posed in the doorway, furious, her lit cigarette tapped repeatedly of ashes it did not possess. "It's a fucking school night. What in the hell have you two been doing?"

"Aw, now," Daddy-o drawled. "We've just been fishing."

"Fishing?" her mother shouted. "For what? For your visitation rights to get yanked?"

Daddy-o flashed his pearlies and gave a shrug that Mabel's mother knew all too well, the one she'd ultimately left him over. A shrug that insinuated he didn't know, didn't care, didn't see what all the fuss was about.

"Don't tell me he got you wrapped up in his hocus-pocus." Mabel's mother said after Daddy-o hightailed it back to the Happy Thicket. "Don't tell me you're buying into his BS."

Mabel imagined her mother on one of Daddy-o's cushions. She was using it the wrong way, folded in half under her head while she sprawled in the sun, drunk. "I dunno. Maybe he's on to something," Mabel suggested.

"More like *on* something," her mother said.

"At least he's happy," Mabel dared to say. "At least he's nice."

Mabel's mother crushed out a second cigarette and stood, like Janet Yuri had, nearly nose-to-nose with Mabel. "He's not happy and he's not nice. He only seems that way. Deep down, he's miserable and mean. And he knows just how to string you along."

Mabel thought of the bowie knife and the felt-tip mustache on her mother's photo. Then she listened as her mother went outside to swear and smoke, then cry and sob. Mabel closed her eyes until she was back above the pond. This time, by herself, she made it almost up to where the clouds looked like rain.

*

At school on Friday, Janet Yuri watched Mabel the way the Happy Thicket owner watched Daddy-o, with suspicion and ire. In English, she passed Mabel a note. It was a drawing of two stick figures, a man and a girl smiling, oblivious, while an asteroid hurtled toward them. *Ignorance is bliss!* was written under it in loopy cursive, complete with *i*'s dotted with daisies.

"Your dad coming to pick you up today?" Janet asked after class.

"What's it to you?" Mabel answered.

"I want to meet him, is all," Janet said. "Who wouldn't want to meet The World's Happiest Man?"

Mabel frowned, protective. "I'm walking home alone," she said. "He won't be here."

But he was. There, after school, on the fence—once again a snagged autumn leaf clinging hopeful—was Daddy-o, eating a vanilla soft serve with his left hand and dangling a necklace through the chain-link with his right.

"I made you this, Maybe Baby. Made it for you today."

Janet Yuri stormed Mabel as Mabel stormed the fence. "Get in the van," Mabel seethed to her father. "Get in the van *now*."

But Daddy-o didn't flinch. He just kept on with his cone, while Mabel snatched the leather necklace from him. It was a choker sporting a small metal oval, likely cut and sanded from an old beer can, an oval that was stamped with the words CAN DO.

"This your dad?" Janet asked.

"I'm her dad," Daddy-o replied.

"I hear you're lots of fun to be around," Janet said.

"That's what they tell me." Daddy-o smiled.

"Then why don't you take me and Mabel to get some of that ice cream?"

"No," Mabel cried. "Absolutely not."

"Now, Mabel," Daddy-o said. "That's not how we talk to guests."

"You two can go," Mabel said. "I will not." Daddy-o winked and climbed into the yellow van. Janet Yuri scaled the fence and did as well. Daddy-o's dogged commitment to friendliness suddenly felt like betrayal. Mabel groaned and climbed the chain-link. "Make it fast," she said, as she got into the van. "I have work to do."

*

At the Dairy Queen, Mabel turned hot and silent when Daddy-o produced his beaded pouch of dimes to buy Janet a cone. She knew her father had likely cleaned three toilets to pay for the ice cream. Janet asked for sprinkles.

"So, Mabel tells me you're never sad. That nothing, not a person, place, or thing can bring you down."

"Mabel says that, does she?" Daddy-o smiled at Mabel.

"Sure does." Janet licked her cone. "How come she doesn't take after you?"

Mabel clenched her jaw. "Stop it, Janet."

"What do you mean?" Daddy-o said.

Janet tilted her head in false concern. "I'm worried about Mabel. Mabel passes me notes." Janet reached into her pocket and produced a wad of folded paper. "Like these."

Mabel reached across the table, but Daddy-o swiped the notes away with cheer. "My girl's a writer," he said. "I love me some Mabel."

Daddy-o opened the first. It was one Janet had drawn of a stick figure girl in a hangman's noose. The second was of a stick figure girl in a car careening off a cliff. The third was of a girl with x's for eyes and a knife in her chest. The caption read: *What's the point? Here's the point!*

Janet licked her cone, around and around, with precision. "I find them troubling."

Daddy-o stared at the three notes as if he were learning to read. "What," he said softly. "How?"

Mabel, raw and fuming, said nothing. She did not understand how notes that were not hers could make her feel so exposed. Maybe Janet was right. Maybe Mabel was a liar. And maybe Daddy-o—who sat quiet across the table, his face now drained of its Pensacola brown—was too.

"I thought you should know," Janet said. "I thought maybe . . ."

Daddy-o did not stay to hear the rest. He rose from the table as if his body hurt. He walked to the door of the Dairy Queen as if the floor were made of ice. And then he got into his yellow van and drove away.

"He doesn't seem that happy to me," Janet said.

Mabel didn't answer her. She closed her eyes and let herself float. Up over the table where she saw the white part in Janet's black hair. Up through the red roof of the restaurant. Up over the winding road that led to the Happy Thicket Motor Lodge. She needed to see where Daddy-o was going, where Daddy-o had gone.

*

Up close, the spotted fawn on the Happy Thicket Motor Lodge sign was much bigger than Mabel had imagined. From the ground, it had looked like the size of a leaping squirrel, but in reality, it was as large as a prancing dairy cow, fashioned of painted metal and surrounded by a mass of neon tubes that flashed the deer's three-part escape: before, during, after. It was nearly big enough for Mabel and Daddy-o to climb on and pretend to ride, rodeo-style. They'd been up on the sign since the Dairy Queen, standing side by side in silence and watching the sky go from light blue to dark blue.

Mabel finally spoke. "I didn't write those notes."

"But you feel that way," Daddy-o said.

"Sometimes," Mabel said. "Sometimes not."

On the edge of the motor lodge's sign, fifty feet up in the air or more, Daddy-o and Mabel held hands. The lights hummed like a colossal swarm of gnats and turned the two of them red, yellow, green. Red, yellow, green. *Stop, think, go. Stop, think, go.*

Below, Mabel could see a fire truck, two police cars, and an ambulance. The motel's proprietor leaned against Daddy-o's yellow van like he'd been waiting for this. The firefighters brought out a life net—it looked to Mabel like a large, dotted hoop, a giant dream-catcher—which they hauled to the base of the sign. They squinted up in the night at Daddy-o and Mabel. Mabel thought she saw Janet in the gathering crowd. Daddy-o pointed out who he thought was Mabel's mother.

"The girl should go first," a fireman called through a mega-phone. "First, the girl!"

Daddy-o winked at Mabel. His teeth shone bright as bathroom tiles. "Can you?" he asked. "Can you go first, Maybe Baby?"

Mabel nodded and beamed. She touched the hollow of her

throat where the silver disk of Daddy-o's necklace rested. "Can," she said. "Can do!"

"Then show them," Daddy-o said. "Show them how it's done."

Mabel squeezed her eyes shut. Then Mabel opened them wide. Then Mabel leapt off the sign, just like a deer, *the* deer, and out into the night, in three robotic flashes, scaling the smiling log to land in the night sky. "I can!" she called to Daddy-o. "I did!"

Mabel galloped through the cool black. Above where the trees, now sleeping, blushed with fall. Beneath where the clouds, now hiding, swelled with rain. Below, she could hear the crowd gasp, a fireman shout, a siren cry a single cry. She laughed until her cheeks shone with tears. And at one point, she looked back to see if Daddy-o would join her, out where nothing and no one could bring her down.

THE PUPIL

AFTER SCHOOL, TO escape my Uncle Drake and his collarbone jabs, I like to climb up on the roof of Mom's and my straw-colored house with a fresh pack of Luckies and a cream soda. Where the crappy back porch juts out from our cracker box, there's a small shingled ridge I can straddle like a bronco, slide my sneakers into the gutters like stirrups, and pretend to gallop my sorry self out of this place. Up on the roof, I get a wide view of the world I don't understand anymore—where the dust-colored plains rush toward a sky that backs away, hands up, the same way Mom does, surrendering against the kitchen wall, when Drake has too much to drink and even more to say. Up here, I can see the desperation of the Oklahoma landscape, how it tries to offer up something worth looking at—just like the homely girls do in the parking lot of the 7-Eleven—but most of the time the sad view falls flat: a distant patch of houses that seem stuck into the earth by old television antennae, a wind-beaten stand of crippled cottonwoods, or that dark skid in the road, where the highway turns toward Enid. That charcoal line the rain won't wash away; that mark I can touch with the tip of my cigarette, out there, where they found my dad's motorcycle. A place about two hundred feet from where he landed.

Drake hasn't caught on to the fact that I sit up here. Sometimes, when he comes out to the backyard to shoot starlings with his slingshot, I'm still on the roof, a phantom cowboy he can't see. I can hear the things he says to himself: who owes him money, who's worthless, where he's gonna tell someone to go. He paces the yard, like he's in a courtroom, his bald head, white and shiny with two lines of lavender stubble over each ear, as bold as a moonlit honeydew. From up here, I find out what he thinks of me: *soft*. And what he thought of my dad: *softer*.

Things were better before Drake came along with his dented suitcase and bottle of strawberry Boone's looking for a place to shower and shit. Mom's mouth didn't stay all screwed up like a cat's behind. She didn't get short with me for leaving my Jockeys on the floor or for drinking straight from the carton. She brought me Butterfingers from the vending machine at work, did that little something with her bangs that looked fresh. Now she's just sagging down like our gutters from her mooch of a brother and his wet-leaf attitude. He's stocked our freezer with Stouffer's, parked his truck on our pansy bed, put a big oily stain on the headrest of my dead father's recliner.

At night, Drake watches *Wheel of Fortune* while Mom boils him a bag of creamed chipped beef. He picks his cuticles with a pocketknife and sits with his feet spread wide, his unlaced boots sticking out their leather tongues at me. I know he's got something other than *Wheel* on his mind. Don't think the irony that the show is really a glorified version of hangman is lost on me. My uncle can think of plenty of people he'd like to see strung up, from the hippies and the Commies to Carter. Personally, I think Drake's in a cult. Not the kind that worries itself with comets or Kool-Aid or cornfields. The kind that sticks to the basics. The kind that thinks that God'll only bless America when it's as straight and white as a shower-curtain rod.

Mom says it's good for a boy my age to have a man his age around our two-bit house. Says it'll teach me the ins and outs of manhood. I say screw Drake. Don't keep him around on account of my hairless dick. I'd be better off with a dog. That's all I ever asked for anyway. And maybe some Saturdays at Radio Shack where I can use the remote-control cars without having to buy them.

Drake plays like he knows a lot. When we sit around the glass-top table, he puts his greasy hands all over where Mom Windexed and talks like it went out of style with his ex-wife's rack. He yammers about interest rates and bass fishing and how Oklahoma has too many Cherokee and how to install a ceiling fan, which he has yet to do. He eats off Mom's plate, wipes his face from forehead to chin with a paper towel at the end of the meal. He tells me what I need to do with my life, saves that for dessert. Over tapioca he gets bossy.

"See, what this boy needs, Eileen, is direction."

"That's right," I say. "Direction outta town."

Drake flicks my earlobe with his pudding spoon. "That's what I'm getting at, Sis. Mickey here'll smart-ass you straight to hell when you ain't looking."

So, Drake signs me up for some derelict day camp. Summer's coming in. Leaves are shooting out like bright green fly-rod feathers on the tops of the trees. The asphalt smells as strong as moth balls by the bus stop. And by ten o'clock, it's hot enough for me to start stinking ripe in algebra where I watch Joe Yutt watch Patricia Smurt and wish it was the other way around. Drake says once school's out, I'll be spending my time at the Bar None Ranch for Boys. Some dust patch ten miles out of town that specializes in fixing dopes that've gotten too big for their britches. He's done the research, he tells Mom. There'll be manual labor, farm animals to tend to, healthy competition.

*

Drake's as wrong about the camp as he is in the head. The other boys don't seem all that troubled to me. Mostly just bored guys who've taken to slouching since their foreheads went greasy. I've only seen one switchblade and two *Playboys* and for the most part, the humidity keeps everyone in the shade talking about tits and carburetors. Most days we just get out of running laps by hiding behind a broken-down Partridge Family–looking bus and smoking butts we find crushed in the tire treads. Sometimes we dig a hole for what they say'll be a new pool. Sometimes we kick a ball around that's as soft and useless as an old udder. And the farm animals are nothing more than some goats that'll ram you if you don't give up your Doritos fast enough.

I play like I'm interested in the things the guys concern themselves with: pacing out a baseball diamond, bragging on how to hot-wire a car, claiming I've seen a girl's privates in the light of day. But the old swimming pool's what calls my name, even though it's got a thin slime of slippery green all around the vinyl liner and no slide to speak of. I spend most of my time there, under the charge of a fatty named Troy, who's got a glass eye and a goiter and shows me how to clean the filters.

"Gotta pull them leaves up and out, up and out," he says, like it's some kind of calculus problem. "Reach in there good, Mickey, and pull them leaves up and out."

I'm there mostly for the rodents. I found a bloated weasel one day, a slick chipmunk the next, a waterlogged squirrel like a girl's wet ponytail down by the drain yesterday. As interesting looking as they are drowned, I prefer to find them alive. To reach in with that long, rusted net and strain them out like macaroni, flip them over a fence where they can dry out in the ragweed and catch their breath. Nothing worse than thinking about them swimming all night. Treading water by the light of the moon, scraping their tiny claws against the green sides. That really gets to me. So, I try to find Troy first thing in the morning. Last Thursday I gave my Cheetos to a rabbit that'd been doing laps for who knows how long.

Troy's as ugly as they come. His one good eye is as dumb as a cow's, and his fake one just stares out at nothing like a swirly planet I should know by now. Sometimes he takes out his glass eye when he swims. Just pops it out like a little wet saucer and puts it in a groove on the picnic table. I watch the eye while it watches Troy while Troy watches the backs of boys playing Wiffle ball as he floats around like a colorless turd in the Oklahoma sun.

*

My father had a green thumb. "He could grow anything," my mother sometimes says. "Except a pair," Drake always says back. In our backyard, you can still see where the old tomato plants laced themselves around the wire fence, the black vines of last year snagged like dead snakes. My dad could grow tomatoes as big as grapefruits, as red as blood. "They're just like people, Mickey," he'd say. "The more bullshit you feed them, the stronger they end up." Sometimes he'd eat them straight from the garden, like apples. He carried a saltshaker in his pocket from July to September and when he saw a ripe one, he'd just pluck it right from the vine and start tapping out some table salt on it before a rabbit or squirrel could beat him to it. "Your dad is weird as hell," a friend once said, looking out my bedroom window. "You're weird as hell," I repeated that night to my dad. "Everyone says so." My mother had cried at that. Right there at the dinner table, with her face in her palms like I'd finally learned the truth. But my dad didn't flinch. In fact, he apologized. He said sorry, plain and calm, then ate the rest of his meal in peace. Then he said it again as he washed the dishes and again before bed. My father said sorry enough times that night to convince me he was wrong and everyone else was right.

*

Drake asks me how everything's panning out over at Bar None. I don't tell him the place'd be better named Bar Nothing-to-Do 'cause he'd quit paying the fifteen dollars a day to send me there. I just tell him we're digging an Olympic-size pool and that I've learned to lasso a heifer. I tell him my counselor makes us eat dirt if we cop out on our push-ups. I tell him I had to run a mile with a cement block duct-taped to my back. I probably shouldn't exaggerate. It just makes Drake think he's the best thing since sliced pizza and it makes my mother fill that beanbag ashtray on her knee with one half-smoked Misty after another. But I like going. I like getting up every day at six and walking to the 7-Eleven where the sawed-off bus comes to pick me and a bunch of losers up. I like the early morning, the way the creeping heat feels like a word on the tip of my tongue, the way a Lucky Strike goes with powdered donuts, the way no one says a thing as the bus bounces through the cotton-woods like a rusty mattress.

*

Troy's studying to get on *Jeopardy!* He keeps trivia books in the screen house and when the sun gets to his neck and the twelve noon heat rash breaks over the collar of one of his two Hawaiian shirts he starts up with the flash cards.

"Did you know George Washington had a dog named Sweet Lips?" He puts bug spray on his toes, says that's where a vampire bat would bite if it had the chance. His breasts hang low like a woman's. "Or that Teddy Roosevelt had a guinea pig named Father O'Grady and a snake named Emily Spinach?"

Troy pinches himself into an old lawn chair, lets his swim trunks ride up tight around his groin in a way that looks like torture. He licks his thumb to peel through the cards, sweats like he's breaking a fever. Something about him is too damn kind. I eat Raisinets slow in the shady stench of sunscreen and wonder if Troy has ever been laid.

"Calvin Coolidge," Troy offers, "had his head rubbed with Vaseline while he ate breakfast in bed."

I don't clue Troy in that this sort of bullshit isn't on *Jeopardy!* "What else?" I say.

He tells me that rats and horses don't vomit, that rubber bands last longer if refrigerated, that during an hour's swim at a municipal pool, the average person ingests a half liter of urine.

"Is ours a municipal pool?" I ask.

"No," Troy says. "And don't make it one."

I look out at the other guys playing football. It's supposed to be touch, but all I see is tackle. One kid's face has been rubbed in the dust so he looks like the kind of person Drake would strangle. Troy takes a dainty sip from a thermos. I bet my chocolate raisins he knows how to knit.

"And believe it or not," Troy continues, "the closest relative to the *Tyrannosaurus rex* is the common chicken."

I snort, flick three candies out to melt on the concrete like rabbit pellets, hope to attract some ants that'll have Troy spraying Raid like a nervous housewife. "That's a crock," I respond.

"No," Troy says, holding up a card. "It's true."

"Who gives a shit?" I ask.

"*Language*," Troy reminds. "And I do," he adds. "I give a shoot."

*

Drake says I look awful pale for a boy who's outside all day. I tell him we're painting the inside of a barn. That I spend all my time up in the rafters with a can of whitewash trying to breathe through the bird crap. That I'm lucky I haven't died from histoplasmosis. He says that sounds productive, but then he frowns; something in his eyes glints a warning at me, a flash of minnow on muddy brown. "And who's teaching you big words like that?"

I shrug. He leans back in the rocker and stares at me for a second, burning a red ring of humiliation around my neck.

*

Troy tells me Winston Churchill was born in a ladies' bathroom, that the spiny anteater is the only animal that doesn't experience REM sleep, that two-thirds of the world's eggplant is grown in New Jersey. I tell him I found a garter snake in the filter that looked a hell of a lot like last week's lawnmower belt and that we're running low on chlorine tablets. He puts a hand on my shoulder and thanks me for being responsible. His thumb thinks twice about touching my earlobe—the same one Drake went at with the tapioca spoon. Troy's real eye is dulled by something he won't mention, but his fake one looks like the circle of green vinyl pool when you're down at the bottom looking up at the sun. A place where you go to be born or die. I feel an itching in my gut, like I've eaten fire ants for breakfast, so I go kick around the deflated ball for a while with the other boys and make sure to find the smallest kid and rub his face in the mud.

*

Drake's got himself a new slingshot and a bunch of beads that look like the pie weights Mom used to use when she baked instead of boiled. He sits in the backyard before dinner and kills starlings.

"Did you know," he says, "these birds aren't even from America? The Chinese shipped 'em over here, Mickey. Them and the egg roll."

He takes one down with a plump thud. It flutters a dying wing like Patricia Smurt flutters her tongue around a pencil in algebra class, the way Troy does his eyelashes when the sunscreen drips low.

"What does that tell you about going where you don't belong?" Drake picks up the bird by its legs, shows me where his white marble cracked its gut, and launches it into Mrs. Pitkin's yard with one high arc where it lands on her charcoal grill.

Dinner is served, I think.

*

Troy only touches me on the shoulder. You can tell his thumb thinks about the ear, but it's too shy to try. I go through pool manuals and circle chutes and ladders with a furred-up ballpoint while he rattles off numbers that don't mean crap. *293 ways to make change for a dollar. 119 grooves on the edge of a quarter. 345 pounds of pressure to crack a macadamia nut.*

"And get this," Troy says. "American Airlines saved forty thousand dollars in one year by eliminating one olive in each salad."

"Who eats olives anyway?" I say. Then I feel Drake looking over my shoulder, even though he's not around. "Queers. That's who."

Troy swallows hard and shuts his eyes like a bullfrog. He's stored up lots of words for his neck to get that swollen. When he opens his eyes, the glass one looks sad as hell. Out the hazy green window, I can see three boys smacking a goat on the ass with the yellow Wiffle ball bat. It glows like a sword in the hot midday sun. I tear out a picture of the most expensive swimming pool slide, wad it up, and throw it at Troy who blinks only one of his eyes.

"Fuck," I say.

Troy frowns, puts down his cards, leans out of his mildewed lawn chair to touch me on the shoulder. "Is something on your mind?" he says. "Is there something you want to tell me?"

I look sideways at his hand, splotchy, like he spilled bleach on it. I see his thumb think about my ear. I bolt from the screen house and head for the goat pen where I grab the black one by its stunted horns, two hard thumbs that jab up at heaven, and try to take it down.

*

Patricia Smurt starts showing up at the 7-Eleven at night. In just three weeks she's gone big and soft in the top and rear, and when she leans on the windows of cars to talk to guys two years older, her miniskirt rides up to show the beginning of a backside that's no longer my age. She pours vodka in her Slurpee, laughs like she's being filmed.

Later, on the roof, I think about pinning her down, my knees on her shoulders, my crotch on the center rosebud of her bra, the one I can see when she bends down to pick up used lottery tickets. I'd like her to smack me, just once, so I'd know I was real. Then I'd like her to smack me again, to prove I'm a fake. I take a long drag off my Lucky, and I gaze in the dark to where the highway's

charcoal skid must be. I wonder if my dad is still there, trapped in
time, looking down at his motorcycle and shaking his head. I bet
he doesn't even know he's gone. I bet he just keeps looking at his
motorcycle and shaking his head and wondering how he's going
to fix the mess it's in, a scene rewound and replayed for eternity.
I see him, hands on his hips, fuming and frustrated on the gravel
shoulder looking up to the sky, then back toward the house to that
tiny pinpoint on the roof, where my cigarette glows orange and I
pretend he mistakes it for Mars. I raise my left hand off the shingles, my palm facing out toward him, and I think about waving
him home, waving him on.

*

Drake's taken down eleven starlings since he brought home the
slingshot. I think of that poem, four and twenty blackbirds baked
in a pie. I'd like to make Drake eat what he kills. His eyes have
changed, too. Now there are schools of mean minnows flashing
around on black silt. He yells during *Wheel*. Calls Vanna a whore,
calls Sajak a faggot. I take that as my sign to leave and go to the
7-Eleven where I sit by the newspaper stand with a cold root beer
in my crotch and watch Patricia Smurt straddle the bicycle rack
while she giggles to jocks and throws her hair around like a hooker.
Nights, I keep dreaming that Patricia Smurt's blue raspberry tongue
shows up in the pool filter and Troy won't let me keep it. I dream
that Drake shoots Troy's hand off my shoulder, then tosses it on
Mrs. Pitkin's grill.

*

Troy says he's almost done studying. He knows that peanuts are
an important ingredient in dynamite, that every child in Belgium

is required by law to take harmonica lessons, and that the shortest complete sentence in the English language is *I am.*

"I am," he says. "*I am.* The shortest darn sentence, Mickey. Isn't that something? I am."

I don't say anything. I clean three leaves out of the filter and try to imagine them on Patricia Smurt in the Garden of Eden, but all I can see is Troy out the corner of my eye going through his flash cards like the nicest damn kid in school. I eat my lunch alone under a cottonwood. Something's itching at my gut again. Like there were sparks in my sandwich. In the distance I can see Troy hunched over something in the grass. Probably looking for a four-leaf clover. I know I could crack off that wandering thumb of his with a snap and use it to hitchhike somewhere other than here.

✳

The itching in my gut won't go away. Lasts through a boiled dinner that I can't eat. Gets worse when Drake takes down a red cardinal with one of his marbles and lays it on the lawn chair like a sunburned hand. I take off early for the 7-Eleven before Vanna can flip the first *F* of the night. Patricia Smurt's already there, her tongue already baby blue. She gives me the time of day since the jocks have yet to show.

"What say, Mickey Mouse?" She pushes her straw over one perfect tooth.

"I dunno," I say. "Gonna buy some smokes, I guess."

"Oh yeah?" she says. "Why dontcha get yourself a Slurpee while you're in there?"

"I don't like them," I say.

"I can make you like them," she says.

"I doubt it."

"Well," she says, pulling the straw off her tooth and running a blue tongue across her lips. "You ever heard of tryin'?"

The itching in my gut reaches up to my throat and I picture it getting as fat as Troy's. But whatever Patricia pours into my drink seems to help me forget. She says she wants a ride on my bike, sits her big denim ass on my handlebars, and as I pedal to the baseball field, her hair flies back into my mouth and chokes me. She smells like candy and gasoline and thinks everything's worth laughing about.

Behind the bleachers, we pass a car parked in the shade. Night's coming in with a better attitude than the day, and through a daze of gnats, I see what looks like Troy sitting in the car. I think I hear music. I think I see a boy in the passenger seat snapping his fingers and laughing.

"Who's that?" Patricia asks.

"Nobody," I say. "Nobody I ever seen."

But I feel those ants well up in my throat, and then one of my eyes goes blind. And before Troy can look my way, I yell at Patricia to get back on the handlebars. We go down to where a creek used to be before the world ran dry, and before I can catch my breath, Patricia takes off her shirt, shows me a second's worth of that pink rosebud on her bra, and pushes me into the brown dust like I'm the smallest guy on the team.

I see blue tongues in my mind, Wiffle ball bats as gold as swords, feel myself working at the soft green of the pool sides, reaching up to that circle of sun where you go to be born or die. I feel Troy's thumb on my ear and I know something I didn't know before.

After Patricia leaves, I stay down in the creek bed and keep catching a whiff of candy and fuel. I smoke a half pack of Luckies and look up at the stars where I play I can make out a constellation of my dad. I can see him on the motorcycle, two stars for a muffler, three for his grin, and five for the helmet he shoulda been wearing in the first place.

At dawn, I make up my mind like never before and hop the sawed-off bus to Bar None. When I get there, I watch Troy from behind the one good cottonwood, see how he sits pinched in his chair like he's being hugged. Thanks to the night before, there's a new type of smile on his face, one that looks like it belongs in the filter. I wait for him to go look for something up at the so-called lodge, and then I go down to the screen house and stand over his flash cards. I pick them up and hesitate before I fling them above my head.

They go up in the air like a flock of white doves and fall, as if shot from the sky, onto the surface of the pool. And then, off to the side, I see the picnic table, see how in its third groove rests Troy's glass eye. It's seen me in action. It knows what went down. It's taken it all in without a blink, without squeezing out a tear.

*

The eye feels right in my hand and good in my pocket. It goes with me as I leave the screen house, as I hitchhike back to town, as I pick up my bike from the 7-Eleven where Patricia Smurt pretends not to see me. I feel it at my side, smooth and heavy, as I sit up on the roof of Mom's and my house with Drake's slingshot and wait for the back of his head to appear over the little cement patio after work. Let him ask Mom again if I'm a man or a fag. Let him ask it again as I aim that glass eye and answer, "I am. I am."

STONE FRUIT

O N THE FIRST night of the couple's retreat, Marta was instructed to whip Dean with a silk ribbon while she scolded him for his transgressions. Dean got down on all fours on the olive-green carpet of the Forgiveness Hall and smiled like a Labrador. He liked attention of any kind.

"Bad, Dean, bad," Marta said, monotone. "Shame on you for . . ." Marta paused and searched for something benign to accuse him of, something other than the drinking or the chapter of their relationship Dean referred to as "The Bad Idea" and Marta referred to as "Mackenzie." Marta gave the ribbon an apathetic flick. "Shame on you for leaving the toilet seat up."

Dean feigned remorse and hung his head like a shamed dog. Ventura, their assigned Love Coach, raked his fingers through his short red beard, dissatisfied.

"Try to be emotionally specific, Marta," Ventura said. "For example, when Dean leaves the toilet seat up, how does it make you feel inside?"

Marta twirled the ribbon as if stirring a pot. She wanted to say, *It makes me feel like I need to be less of who I am and more of who*

I'm not, but instead, she said: "It makes me feel like I have to put it down again."

Dean snickered into his sleeve. He was wearing a new flannel shirt, as well as new hiking boots, both of which he'd bought especially for the retreat. "Everyone will know I mean business," he'd explained when he brought them home. "This get-up says, 'that guy is ready to explore the wilderness of love.'"

Marta let her shoulders sag and the ribbon fall. It coiled at her feet like a passive, pink worm. "Tell you what," Ventura said. "Let's take a five-minute break. You know: inhale, exhale? Regroup, reconvene?"

Dean sat back on his haunches. Marta stared blankly past the two men, out the window and beyond the front meadow of the retreat to the remote-control airfield across the road. Earlier that day on the way to Forever Together Couples' Retreat, Marta and Dean had passed the abbreviated runway, where a crowd gathered for the takeoff of a model Virgin Airways jet. Dean, delighted, pulled onto the shoulder to stand and watch, while Marta stayed in the car. She sat in the passenger seat with her arms folded across her chest and stared out the windshield to make it look like she wasn't interested. If Dean thought she was interested, he'd think she was happy, and if he thought she was happy, he'd think his work here was done.

Outside the station wagon, the miniature jet buzzed up and away. Dean hooted in boyish approval. Marta sat and considered the lone wing of a dragonfly they'd hit somewhere in the middle of Indiana. It was stuck to the glass with its own green blood, but still flapped in the wind, frantic, like it had a shot at getting where it needed to be. Marta knew if she was too cold, Dean would find another Mackenzie, but if she was too warm, Dean would grow thick with self-satisfaction—dense with denial—and Marta would never get at what she wanted: the hard pit inside him. Past his perma-smile and Santa laugh, past his burly arms and baby blues, Dean harbored a stone that needed extracting. When Marta was playful and easy, the stone receded further within. But when Marta meant business, it rose to the surface to meet her, just beneath Dean's breastbone.

Once, early in their relationship, Dean had nearly handed it to Marta. It had been on their third date, after a late night of whiskey and errant hands, and back at Marta's place, Dean had picked her up like a child and pressed her deep into the bed. Above her, he looked like he might cry or die, and in response, Marta had put her hands over his heart. That was when she'd felt it, the dark stone of despair rising up and out of him and almost within grasp. She had cupped it beneath her palm as if trapping an insect and Dean had recoiled, but it had almost burst from him. Marta had almost held the real Dean in her hand. That, however, had been three years ago, at the beginning, when risk and romance were the same thing. Now, the only proof the stone still existed in Dean was the way he drank, which was hard and often—a boot heel pressed on the very thing Marta desired.

"That plane was a perfect replica." Dean climbed into the car in a wave of humid air. He smelled of dry grass and metallic sweat. "I mean, they must have to get permission from the FAA to fly those things. I think its wingspan was at least twelve feet."

Marta looked in the sky at the retreating toy. "No way," she said. "It can't be that big."

Dean started the car. "It was. I saw it. All the planes up on that ridge were that big. They were this big." He stretched his arms out across the front seat. "Bigger even. They were big enough to carry house cats."

This struck Marta as funny, but she tried not to show it. "That doesn't seem possible."

"Well, I know what I saw. And I saw cat planes. They're flying above us right now, Marta. Planes full of cats." Dean turned on the AC to dry the sweat from his face. "Planes full of cats full of peanuts."

Marta giggled despite herself, and Dean, encouraged, leaned over to her, hot and hungry. He put his big hands on either side of her face and kissed her. Then he pulled back and looked her in the eyes, earnest for only a flash, before eyeing her pout, her breasts, her waist. "I don't see what all we have to fix," he said, running his hand back and forth over her lap. "But I've got the boots for the job."

Earlier that afternoon, in the front seat, Marta hadn't wanted to give Dean the inch that he would make into a mile, but she'd relented and kissed him back. An inch from Marta, she'd figured, was a mile away from Mackenzie. And now, here they were, circling back.

Dean stood up from the olive-green floor and roused Marta from her thoughts. "I know what we can do in five minutes." He smiled. "See a coat closet around these parts, my lady?"

Marta didn't answer. She walked to the front window of the Forgiveness Hall and stared out the window. She could see another plane taking off across the road, rising like an X in the pink evening sky. From her angle, she couldn't tell if it was toy-sized or life-sized.

Dean came up behind her. "Planes full of cats full of peanuts," he whispered. Marta didn't move. Dean's chest against her back was as thick as a shield. Inside him, the stone was sinking deeper, a lead ball dropped into the sea.

*

The first time Marta saw the Fincastles exchange stones, she thought she might be hallucinating. It was, after all, only a month after her father left—six months to the day after her brother's death—and the phase she'd been going through was nothing short of troubling. Her new hobbies included playing tic-tac-toe on her forearm with an X-Acto knife, pulling the school fire alarm nonchalantly on her way to the girls' room, eating still-frozen pancakes for breakfast, lunch, and dinner. She'd also taken up sleeping in the bathtub, covered in bath towels, and clutching a dry bar of Dial like a teddy bear. So when, one Wednesday night from her bedroom window, she saw her neighbor Lucas Fincastle pry what looked like an apricot kernel from his wife Florence's sternum, Marta thought for sure she'd completely lost her marbles.

But then, the following Wednesday, it happened again. Marta was in bed with the lights off, staring out her window at the Fincastles' house trying not to think of her brother's car and the cliff and the sound her mother had made after the phone call, when Lucas and Florence entered the honey glow of their bedroom, sat down facing one another on the pink quilted bedspread, and reached out reverent palms to one another's chests. Marta sat up, curious. She fumbled for her glasses. The Fincastles closed their eyes and breathed in unison. After a minute or two, they grew vibrant and bright, nearly violet in tone, before throwing back their heads in ecstasy and plunging their hands into one another's hearts.

When it was all over and their eyes were open and Marta, agape, gripped her windowsill equally terrified and turned on, Lucas and Florence both held a glossy brown stone the size of a billiard ball. The Fincastles took turns sniffing the stones, turning them this way and that, and rubbing them over their tear-stained cheeks. After some time, they held the stones up like cocktails and toasted one another. Then they caught each other's gaze and flung the stones to the floor, grabbing one another in desperation. Lucas pressed Florence's face to his own like she was his last, good hope. Florence clawed at Lucas's back and buttocks as if set on devouring him. A lamp was kicked over. A series of ecstatic screams ensued. Marta removed her glasses and stepped away from the window. These were not the neighbors she knew from over the fence, the bird-bath-and-begonias people who had once traded mulching tips with her father. These animals, these Fincastle freaks, were suddenly both monsters and gods. They were everything that Marta—now, for the first time ever—had ever wanted to be.

In the morning, a new day dawned as if nothing extraordinary had taken place. Marta woke and looked at the Fincastles' drawn bedroom window and second-guessed herself. She went downstairs and opened the freezer and brought out three frozen pancakes for breakfast. She took a glass of tap water and her mother's pink pills to her bedside. And then, back in her room, set on a game of tic-tac-toe, she saw them, out the window, the two brown stones, perched with toothpicks over water jars, on the Fincastles' side porch. They glowed like polished mahogany in the morning sun, and Marta stared at them until they stared back—the sad, soulful, brown eyes of God.

Over the course of the next two weeks, Marta watched the stones sprout, then grow, into a pair of intertwining, spindly palms, each with a white, wheel-sized blossom that smelled of sex and citrus. And over the course of the next six months, Marta watched the Fincastles repeat their ritual nearly thirty times, each time appearing to grow not only closer in love, but to some sort of universal truth, as well. Their eyes and bodies glowed with an inner light that Marta came to assume was wisdom, materialized. By the time Marta's father seduced his chiropractor and Marta's mother had her stomach pumped, the Fincastles' porch was a jungle, the Fincastles' lives seemed complete, and Marta, the spectator, sensed something brown and round taking hold within herself.

*

That night, at Forever Together's orientation dinner, Marta and Dean sat with a couple named Alex and Alex. They were of indeterminate gender, both dressed in white, and both with short hamster-colored hair and triangular sideburns. When Marta looked at them across the table, she thought of two saltshakers. She thought of a life without pepper. She felt a flicker of envy for what it must be like to love someone so similar to yourself.

"So, *Alex* and *Alex*," Dean said with emphasis, as if pointing out to Alex and Alex that they shared the same name. "What do you two do for fun?"

Alex and Alex looked at one another and then at Dean.

"That's why we're here," the one on the left said. "We've forgotten how to have fun."

"Yes," the one on the right agreed. "What Alex said."

Marta could see Dean was trying to contain himself, so she mashed her foot on top of his beneath the table.

"Well," Dean said. "What did you *used* to do for fun?"

The Alexes shrugged in unison, like two synchronized swimmers. "We don't remember," they said.

Dean looked down at his bean cakes and radish salad. The retreat had cost nine hundred dollars and Marta could tell this was what he was thinking about.

"We come here every year," one Alex said. "Which means it's either working . . ."

"Or it's not," the second Alex said.

Marta picked up a piece of parsley and twirled it between her fingers. "Well, we're here because . . ."

"Because I have too much fun," Dean interrupted.

Marta frowned and opened her mouth but nothing came out. Dean took a big gulp from his water glass. Marta watched him drink, then she narrowed her eyes. Somewhere nearby, perhaps in one of his new hiking socks, there was a flask.

"See, Alex and Alex," Dean went on, "according to Marta, she lives on the Island of Reality and I live on the Island of Denial. You know, Destination Head-in-the-Sand. Marta thinks I'm not facing my demons and, truth be told, Alex and Alex, I don't have any demons except her."

Marta felt as if she'd been slapped. Normally when Dean drank, he became ridiculous and she became surly. She leaned forward at the table to defend herself when she noticed Dean's flannel shirt was unbuttoned one button more than usual. Right in the center of his chest, just above the first buttoned button, something round surged to get out into the light. Marta pressed her lips together.

"Sure," Dean said, "my father was a prick. Maybe even a dick. And my mother was—how to say this nicely—*habitually unreasonable.* Maybe there were some people in my life who even died when I was a kid. Maybe my sister was missing a leg and a teacher touched me where the sun never shined and my dog fell in a well and starved to death." Dean tossed back the remainder of his water. "But these are not things that I carry around with me. I'm a big boy. What's gone is gone, Alex and Alex. There is nothing to unload, so to speak. I am a happy person." Dean jerked a thumb at Marta. "Unless, of course, someone keeps insisting that I'm not a happy person, in which case I may eventually not be one."

Alex and Alex and Marta didn't respond. All three of them looked at Dean and then at their plates. "So. Which Alex is the bad Alex and which Alex is the good Alex?"

"Dean," Marta said.

"No, seriously," Dean said, flopping his fork left and right. "One of you is the wrong one and one of you is the right one. Tell me which one of you is the wrong one, and I'll show you how to have some of that fun you don't know how to have anymore."

Marta had had enough. "I think what Dean's saying is," she interjected, "is that he will introduce you to someone named Mackenzie who has no real opinions or needs. He'll find you someone blank to bone."

Alex and Alex both went wide-eyed and Marta felt instantly ashamed. Dean smirked and shook his head. He brought a bottle of what appeared to be spring water out from under the table and untwisted its top. "No," he said. "What I was going to suggest was that Bad Alex come with me tomorrow. Whichever one of you that is, I'll walk you over to that remote-control airfield across the street where people still know how to enjoy life." Dean took a swig. "For what it's worth, I never boned Mackenzie, Marta. I never boned Mackenzie, Alex and Alex. All I did was talk to her for a while. It was nice to talk to someone who believed me when I said I was happy."

Marta looked at Dean's chest. The lump was visibly growing. She searched for what to say to make it finally emerge. "Pfft." Marta rolled her eyes. "You're not happy, Dean. Alex and Alex, trust me on this. Dean is not a happy person."

Dean banged a fist on the table and the four bean cakes gave a startled jump. His chest bulged. Marta went on. "No one drinks like Dean drinks if they're really happy."

Dean thumped his other fist. "You're to blame for that," he nearly roared.

Marta felt a sharp pain in her heart. "How dare you," she whispered. "How dare you blame me for your refusal to grow the fuck up."

Trembling, the two of them rose to face each other. The entire dining room of Forever Together had fallen into a hush, as if Dean and Marta had been hired to put on a show.

"Growing up, Marta," Dean said, "is not synonymous with growing miserable."

Marta felt weak. She clutched her waist. "I'm not asking you to be miserable, Dean," she whispered. "I'm just asking you to be real."

Alex and Alex clung to one another. Ventura stood off to the side and raked his fingers through his beard, satisfied. Marta gave a cough and fell to one knee. In an unexpected moment of concern, Dean dropped down next to her and put a hand on her shoulder, but Marta removed his hand and put it over her chest. Then she placed her hand on him, right above his first buttoned button and looked him in the eye.

"What's happening?" Dean asked.

"What's supposed to," Marta answered.

For a moment, Dean and Marta simply stared, then without warning, their heads pitched back in violent ecstasy before swinging forward again in unison. With their eyes locked, a noise between groan and moan materialized from Dean. A screech of excruciating pleasure burst from Marta. There was a frozen moment of communal panting, until, frenzied, they plunged their hands into one another's chests and withdrew two shimmering stones. Dean held up Marta's and Marta held up Dean's. His was the size of a grapefruit. Hers was the size of a gumball. Both were the color of polished ebony. Tears poured from Dean and he shook with noiseless sobs. Sweat poured from Marta and she quivered with quiet laughter. Dean handed Marta his stone and he picked her up in his arms. He carried Marta and Marta carried the stones, and glowing they went back to their cabin, followed by the sound of quiet, reverent applause.

*

The next morning, Marta woke to the far-off sound of a plane. She lay in bed and watched out the window, in the apricot sky, for a plane to rise like a silver X above the silhouetted trees. She imagined planes full of cats and smiled. She imagined planes full of cats full of peanuts and laughed. Last night, she'd given herself to Dean as she always did, but for the first time Dean had realized it was not her body she offered, but her soul. Marta rolled over to face Dean, to show him her joy, but he wasn't there. Marta called for him. She crawled from the bed and put on her robe and looked in the bathroom. She looked in the closet. She looked in the tiny sitting room. She peered out the window again to the porch. When Marta realized he was gone, she began looking for the stones. She looked for the grapefruit-sized one and the gumball-sized one. She overturned their suitcases, the trash cans, until panic began to form between her breasts, a fear that was brown and round and ready to begin again.

Marta threw on her unlaced sneakers and burst from the cabin. She ran down the gravel driveway of Forever Together, in her robe and loose shoes, clumsy and emotional. "Dean?" she cried. "Dean! Where are you?"

She passed the cabins where couples sipped coffee and stared, the Forgiveness Hall where Ventura raked his beard. She passed Alex and Alex out on a morning walk. Both were dressed in white and both nodded at Marta as she ran and ran and ran. She ran across the damp front meadow, out the front gate of the retreat, and up the small ridge of the airfield. The morning was almost past the moment where anything was possible. Soon the sun would rise, high and bright, to kill the day's potential. The heat would arrive and things would return to how they always were. Marta crested the small ridge. A plane flew overhead. Marta couldn't tell if it was a toy or real. Further down, at the edge of the runway, Marta saw Dean in the morning mist, looking up. Marta trudged through the last swath of bluegrass to get to him.

"Dean," she said, breathless. "What are you doing?"

Dean didn't look at Marta. He didn't answer her either. He had on his flannel shirt buttoned back to the top, his boots laced and tied. His left hand was jammed deep into the pocket of his shorts. His right hand shielded his eyes from the early sun as he watched the plane gain altitude.

"Have you seen the stones?" Marta said. "Our stones? Please tell me you know where they are."

Dean took a moment, then he pointed to the plane. "They're up there," he said flatly. "In the plane."

Marta stood damp and winded and squinted up at the sky. Then she looked around the runway, down one end and then the other, to see if she could see who was flying the plane. "You can't be serious," she said.

"I'm serious," Dean said. "Like you've always wanted me to be."

Marta choked. "But we need the stones, Dean. We can't get anywhere without them."

Dean took his right hand down from his face and crammed it deep into his other pocket. He shook his head. "That's where you're wrong, Marta. Those stones," he sighed. "We can't get anywhere with them."

Marta looked at Dean and then up at the sky. The two of them stood there watching the plane, Dean with his hands in his pockets, Marta with hers over her mouth in disbelief. The plane whirred, sputtered, returned to whirring, circled and rose, like a plant growing toward the sun. Marta imagined the stones inside it. Her small one and Dean's large one, sprouting, unfurling, intertwining until the plane nearly burst open. She saw wheel-sized blossoms opening up wide and humid against the windows, like lovers' palms pressed. Marta closed her eyes and listened. The plane's whir grew faint and then it returned, it grew fainter still and then returned a second time. She couldn't tell if it was retreating or coming home. She couldn't say if the plane would circle back and land at their feet or disappear before they'd even had a chance to eat breakfast.

Dean held out his hand to Marta. "Ready to go back?" he said.

Marta opened her eyes and searched the sky for the plane's tiny X. She didn't answer Dean. She didn't take his hand. She just stood and waited, straining her eyes and ears, until she hurt all over with love.

THREE COUCHES

S PENCER WAS LEAVING his wife, Cassandra, and their two children, Melody and Levi. Melody was twelve, chocolate-haired, and accomplished on the violin. Her favorite color was mauve, and she found eggs, scrambled or otherwise, revolting. Spencer felt confident that Melody was the sort of girl who'd be prudent and prudish, at least until she was legal. Levi was blond and seven, toothy and not too sharp, bewitched by trucks and trains, transportation in general, as well as ice cream, which he could never manage, whether it came in a cup or cone. Cassandra, well. She was busy. Eternally occupied, rushing, thinking, scratching out and scratching through ballpoint lists, staring off into a place in space that was composed of dental appointments and vaccinations and reupholstery. But still, in the ways that seemed to matter to everyone else, Cassandra was near perfect. He knew it. She knew it. But none of that mattered. Spencer was leaving them, all three of them, with the two-story brick in the good school district so he could move into a one-bedroom apartment in the bad one.

What difference did it make where he lived? It wasn't like he was going to school. He didn't need a science lab that promised no less than one microscope per two students. He wasn't going to get remarried and have more kids who deserved a cap on class size or a cafeteria that composted or a jazz band elective. A one-bedroom that backed up to the reservoir, to a sagging fence woven with wind-blown grocery sacks, was all Spencer required. That and a leather couch and a mattress on cinder blocks and a premiere cable package and a couple of bars of Zest.

Spencer had no use for a plaster birdbath or matching night-stands with brass claw-and-ball feet or a toile camelback sofa like the one he'd been living with for fifteen years. It wasn't like he'd miss the salmon bath towels that advertised *CFW* (her initials, not his) or the tissue box made of mother-of-pearl that held little more than something he was going to snot on. And he could certainly do without the carp-shaped windsock and the perky pineapple flag and Cassandra's "Melody has a tap recital and Levi has a soccer banquet and don't forget that next weekend we promised to go see so-and-so who just gave birth to such-and-such." Spencer was just fine making that whole song and dance go away. The sheer madness of self-made madness had just become more than he could bear. So, Spencer had made up his mind to leave. All he wanted now was to run the num-bers all day and come home at 6:45 to an empty apartment that smelled of old, sculpted shag. He wanted to walk in the door with his Mexican carryout and sit on the couch and watch *Bonanza Gold Diggers* and eat queso and chips and drink warm, dark, Irish beer.

This was an image he played in his mind, on loop, as if it were pornography. He knew he was imagining the classic divorced man, the deadbeat dad. He knew it should bring him some sort of guilt or grief or horror, but all it brought him was relief. When he saw himself on the couch, getting fat, the cheese down the front of his button-down, the dingy walls where someone else's picture hooks still hung, the television on while he slept in his work clothes, beer tipping invisible into the deep shag, it was like a little window into Eden. He could hear the angels sing.

*

Of course, everyone wanted to know why Spencer was leaving. Was there someone else? Was he going broke? Had he lost his job months back? Had he been pretending to go to work all this time while he was really going to a bar all day to drink? Was it pain pills? Was he secretly dying? Was he finally coming out of the closet? The answer was always the same: No, no, no, no, no, no, no.

"Men," his boss informed him, "never leave unless they have a plan. And by *plan* I mean *woman*." But Spencer didn't have a woman. His lover was emptiness. He had nothing outside of his marriage. He had nothing inside of himself. It was as if he'd been erased, hosed down. He knew he loved Cassandra and Melody and Levi, but he couldn't feel it. He knew nothing other than that feeling nothing was wrong. Spencer didn't know how to explain why he was leaving until one day, in counseling, with Cassandra sitting beside him dabbing at her swollen eyes, it came to him. "It's just," he said, then paused, momentarily exhilarated that it had finally dawned on him. "It's just that life isn't what I thought it would be."

There was a brief moment of silence during which Spencer heard a woman laugh, far off, outside in the parking lot. Then Cassandra lurched from the couch, as if someone had stabbed her in the back. She nearly turned over the coffee table that held the Kleenex, the dish of Wint O Green mints, the grimy communal stress ball.

"Well," she said, trembling. "I've officially heard it all." Then she grabbed her purse and her coat and stormed out of the office in a puff of cold air that felt like a flash of death but dissipated soon enough. The therapist waited until she was gone, then he blew air out of his nose in a bullish way.

"Spencer," Dr. Darvin said. "Tell me some things that have turned out the way you expected."

Queso from Durango's, Spencer thought. *Bonanza Gold Diggers.* But Spencer did not say those things aloud.

"Life has a lot of moving parts," the doctor said. "But if we start from love instead of obligation, those parts can be a lot easier to manage."

That made Spencer think of the year he'd played baseball. He'd been ten. He liked the coach. He liked the teammates. He even liked the uniform, the feel of the ball tossed up and down in his glove, the sound of the bat when it made a good connection. But everything put together had seemed a joke. All the parts, when forced to interact, seemed absurd. What was the point, this running from here to there? This line and that line? It was a fabrication. A farce. An orchestrated circus that caused grown men to turn crimson, women to scream nose-to-nose with other women, children to doubt their self-worth. And, one particular May Saturday, after a missed triple, it even caused one man, an opposing coach with a handlebar mustache, to drop to his knees and clutch his heart. At first it seemed a show, a dramatic reaction. Some of Spencer's teammates even pointed and jeered. But when the man keeled over on his forehead in the orange dirt and proceeded to foam at the mouth, it became clear something dire had come to pass. All in the name of something made-up and make-believe.

An ambulance eventually came to cart the coach off, but by the time it arrived, bouncing over the grass, he was purple. Spencer watched the EMTs bend over him, their green latex gloves perched on their hips like exotic birds. He watched them lift the man's limp body onto a stretcher. He watched the ambulance retreat. People stood in the warm sun and murmured. Spencer squinted into the sky until he felt nothing. Then he took off his glove and took off his hat and went to retrieve his bat, until his coach grabbed his elbow and frowned. "The game goes on, Spencer," he said. "It always goes on." And it did. With the same, if not intensified, passion as before.

Spencer wondered if that episode was when his heart had gone blank, watching that opposing coach foam his way to indigo. Sure, Spencer had mustered enough emotion in his later years to court Cassandra and propose to Cassandra the way a practical, math-minded actuary might court and propose, but when things had gotten tough, when the family pandemonium had begun, he'd reverted to squinting into the sky and erasing himself. When his children presented him with frustrating scenarios, when Cassandra laid out her to-do lists on the dining room table, one-two-three-four-five, Spencer could feel apathy coming on like a trance, like a squeegee down a plate glass window. That was when he went through the motions of pretending to care, of pretending to be interested, when what he really wondered was what would life be like if no one did anything. If everyone just got on the floor and curled up together and only rose to use the toilet and to make instant oatmeal. Spencer thought for a moment about voicing this to Dr. Darvin, but instead, he just sat there on the gray couch and thought of the sofa back at the two-story. What had those people on the fabric been doing? He'd stared at them for years while Cassandra sat by his side, in the early years with her laugh and wine, in more recent years with her ballpoint and lists, but now he couldn't recall what those people printed all over the camelback had been up to. Fishing, maybe. Threshing wheat. Spencer couldn't recall and it hurt to try. So, he stood up, helped himself to some Wint O Greens, put on his hat, and tipped it.

*

Spencer thought that going back to the house to say goodbye and pack up his things would be hard on the kids. He felt like it would be a big event, a dramatic exit. So he left the clothes and the kids and Cassandra the same way he left cocktail parties—without saying *so long* or *thank you.* He just went to work one morning and didn't go back home when he was done. On the way to his new apartment, he bought a bar of Zest and a cheap yellow toothbrush and he left everything else back at the two-story. He figured it was thoughtful of him in a way. Cassandra and the kids could slowly get used to him not being there, and then when they got used to that, maybe toward summer, they could go through his closet and empty it out and get used to his clothes not being there either. What else had he really left behind besides some oxfords and khakis? His uncle's war helmet, he supposed. Maybe a set of damp encyclopedias in the basement. A box of Wheat Thins. (He was the only one who ate Wheat Thins.) It wasn't like it was hard to start over. He just needed some basics. Some socks and paper plates. A container of Coffee Mate. Batteries for the remote.

*

Spencer's friends thought he was crazy. They told him as much. Cassandra looked good for her age. She wasn't more than about 130, 135 in the winter. Once or twice a month, she could be a real pill, a borderline bitch, but the rest of the time, she was a doll, sometimes a saint. She had good teeth, a genuine laugh, a way of anticipating the needs of the kids. She still gave it up every week or so, usually in a tired sort of way, but she acquiesced nonetheless. The kids weren't terrors. They had manners enough, a modicum of charm. Regardless, Spencer wanted none of it. He wanted the queso and chips. He wanted the Pearson brothers on Channel 241 running Klondike gravel through their sluice box. He wanted no talking, no folded laundry in the front hall, no obligation to explain the rules of badminton, Clue, the fox-trot, geometry. He saw himself never having to show someone how to ride a ten-speed, how to wind up a rubber hose, how to measure twice, cut once. Never again would he want to put his fist through a wall watching Levi tie his shoes by clumping his shoelaces up in a little pile. Never again would he experience the agony of seeing that nightly lump of toothpaste in Melody's sink. *Did she just let it fall there off her toothbrush? Did she spit it out whole? How much had he spent on these lumps?* Spencer knew it was wrong. There were people out there who had kids dying. Kids hooked up to tubes and bags and pumps. But still: a scooter left behind the wheel of his Camry three or four times a week. It was just one thing after another.

*

On the first morning in the new apartment, Spencer looked out at the reservoir and stretched. He didn't feel anything. Neither remorseful nor refreshed. He just felt nothing. Which was how he wanted it. Before it had always been something.

At work, he ran some numbers, then he had a piece of cake in the break room, then he ran some more numbers. When he went back for a second piece of cake, he ran into Babson, the IT guy, doing the same.

"Good cake," Babson said. "I think it's spice. No one ever makes spice cake anymore."

Spencer just chewed and gave a nod.

"Hey, sorry," Babson said. "About everything going on." He brushed some crumbs from one hand onto the knees of his pants. "I heard around."

Spencer wasn't sure what to say, so he said, "Well. Life's no picnic."

Babson crossed his arms and nodded. "You got that right," he said. "Even a picnic is no picnic. The last time I went on a picnic, I..." Babson trailed off.

"What?" Spencer said.

Babson looked as though he'd been caught reaching for a third piece of cake. "Oh, nothing," he said. "I don't know what I was going to say."

Spencer felt suddenly persistent, almost pushy. "No. You were going to tell me something. Come on. Tell me. Tell a man a story."

Babson raised his shoulders and shook his head. "It's really not that great of a story," he said. "I just came across an animal is all."

Babson paused and Spencer stared in a way intended to make Babson feel obligated. Spencer knew it was out of character for him to act as such. It was the first time he was using his predicament to garner pity, to force a reaction, but he felt an urgent and inexplicable need to know the details of the story. "What kind of animal, Babson?" Spencer asked. He surprised himself by calling Babson by name. He surprised Babson, too.

"It was a cat," Babson said quietly. "Tangled in some wire."

Spencer felt something close to empathy wash over him; he could feel the very wire on his own leg. "Like barbed wire?"

Babson shrugged. "Yeah," he said. "I tried to get him out, but it just made things worse." Babson uncrossed his arms and rubbed his neck. Then he clasped his hands behind him.

"So," Spencer said. "Then what?"

Babson cleared his throat. "I had no choice," he said. "I put it out of its misery."

Spencer held his cake a little higher, intrigued. "Really?" he said. "And how did you do that?" Spencer asked. "How does one go about putting a cat out of its misery?"

Babson gave a weak smile. He looked at the floor, then out the glass door of the break room. He moved in front of the door to block it. "I had no choice," he said again, almost whispering. "It was the right thing to do."

Spencer stood in a way that he normally didn't stand. Unyielding, feet slightly apart, one hand speared in a pocket, the other, paused indefinitely, with the cake out in front of him. Babson looked out the glass door then back at Spencer. "I didn't have anything on me," he said. There was a long pause before Babson spoke again. "It was a picnic, for chrissakes. All I had was a corkscrew."

Spencer stared at Babson for a second to let it sink in. Then he resumed eating his square of spice cake. "Hmph," he said with his mouth full. "Wowf."

Babson ran his fingers through his hair. "I don't know why I brought all this up," he said. "I think I was just trying to make a point, you know. That nothing ever goes perfect in life. Not even a picnic."

Spencer finished his cake. He saw the cat as calico in his mind. He didn't know why, but he felt certain it was a calico. He thought he might ask Babson what the cat looked like, but then he moved past him in a friendly way and said: "Well. Back to work."

By the time he reached his desk, Spencer had made up his mind to go on a picnic. He'd go Saturday, first thing. March wasn't quite picnicking season, but he had his mind set on it. His hope was that he would come across something like Babson had come across. Something that required either saving or slaying. Something that needed mercy. Spencer considered the various ways this could happen: a dog in a well, a duck wrapped in some discarded fishing line, a deer with its legs caught in an old cattle gate. Any of those would suffice.

*

Saturday was cold and royal blue. Spencer woke and dressed in a new pair of jeans and a new gray sweatshirt and a new jacket that featured a little icon of a basketball player dunking. Spencer had never been a basketball fan, but the jacket was something he could buy now that he didn't live with people who would ask him why he'd bought it. He made a cup of instant coffee and while he drank it, he watched the grocery bags in the fence flap in the breeze. Then he went to the nice grocery, the gourmet one that sold baskets and macaroons and French cheese and he bought a basket and macaroons and French cheese. He also bought wine. And a corkscrew. When all that was done, he drove thirty miles out of town until he came to a large swath of land that was maybe part of someone's farm, maybe government land.

Spencer left his car on the gravel shoulder. He climbed over the guardrail and over a fence and he walked until he came to a meadow of dry winter grass tucked between two long stands of walnut and cedar. He spread out his basketball jacket and sat on it. He broke off some of the cheese. He ate a few macaroons. He opened the wine and drank straight from the bottle. He tried to figure out a way to balance the bottle without it tipping over, but it was too precarious, so he had no choice but to drink it all. After a while, he lay back and closed his eyes. It was cold, but he tried to imagine what kind of animal he might come across in a plain place like this.

Maybe a coyote or a dairy cow. Maybe a hawk dragging a broken wing. Spencer went in and out of sleep. He felt he was attached to a balloon. He felt he was lodged in a deep crack in the earth. He felt he could not remember his name. Then something came into view. It was the toile camelback couch from the two-story. There in the cold field in his half sleep, he saw what the people printed on it were doing. It was a story. Of a family. Of a woman with apples in her lifted apron. Of two children, a girl tying ribbons in a pony's mane, a boy sailing a boat with some sort of stick. There was also a man, leaning against a towering elm and playing a flute. It was the sort of world where a father might go out into the world, smiling and properly dressed, and buy his children something. A ball, a kite, or better yet, a cat. It was the sort of sunlit universe where there was little to do. Where the wind never rose above a breeze. Where a husband might show up on his old doorstep and press the doorbell and present his family with a kitten. It was a world where nothing had to be explained. Gifts could just be presented and the presenter could stay or leave. There were no obligations.

At this, Spencer woke fully. He sat up and looked around. The sky was no longer blue but white. He gathered the empty bottle and the cork and corkscrew, the tin of macaroons, what was left of the cheese. He put the things back in the basket. He stood and put on his jacket. Then he walked out of the field and up to a small hill. In one direction, he could see his car, in the other he could see where he had just been. He closed his eyes and saw himself buying the cat. He saw himself ringing the doorbell. He saw himself handing the cat to Melody and Levi. He saw their joy and Cassandra's sorrow. Then he saw himself leaving. He saw himself leave again and again, over and over. Going from his old house to his new couch until it, too, was completely worn out.

LONELYHEARTS

L ENORA'S FIRST HEART arrived in a box of Rice Krispies. It fell into her cereal bowl with a damp thud, and for a brief moment she mistook it for a hunk of roast beef. It was crimson in spots and silver in others—as if it had touched a hot skillet—but when Lenora, startled, splashed it with some 2%, the heart turned an all-over vivid fuchsia and fully came to life.

It twitched off a few grains of puffed rice and sputtered for a time, its veins and arteries unfurling like bean sprouts. When it finally found its bossa nova, it thumped the cereal bowl clear across the table and onto the floor, where the bowl shattered. The heart escaped, dancing out of the kitchen and into the hall, where Lenora trapped it with an overturned spaghetti strainer, the way she might secure a loose hamster.

Lenora bathed the heart in the kitchen sink. She washed the cereal from it with care, as well as some dust and lint and two fragments of cereal bowl. When she was done, Lenora set the heart on a potholder and stared. Its beat was now serene, and Lenora, single and childless, felt a rush of self-satisfaction she had always assumed was reserved for the married or maternal. She retrieved her old fishbowl and filled it with tap water and three iron tablets.

She added six drops of red food coloring. She placed the heart in the bowl and the bowl on her bedside table. By bedtime, its beat had synced with hers. It was better than a pet. Maybe even better than a baby or husband.

*

Lenora's second and third hearts arrived as a pair on her front stoop, in a Styrofoam box packed with dry ice and marked as fresh seafood. These two hearts were smaller and pinker, and not content in glass bowls. They only kept beating when Lenora let them perch on her shoulder like lovebirds, so she let the hearts have their way. When Lenora had to leave the house, she put the hearts into the refrigerator, where the cold, at first, sent them into a temporary hibernation, and she was able to go to the bank, the dentist, the grocery. But after a while, this tactic lost its effectiveness, and the two tiny hearts, furious when abandoned, wreaked havoc inside the fridge, smashing the butter flat and spilling soy sauce and ketchup. Eventually, Lenora let the two hearts perch on her shoulder all day. She went out less. She worked from home. She let a tooth nag her for longer than a tooth should nag someone. Lenora became a hermit, but she also became necessary.

*

The next ten hearts came into Lenora's life in quick succession. In her mailbox, a giant brown heart. In her backyard, a violet one under a fern. On the hood of her rarely used car, a dried-out specimen that required an hour of compressions. Bewildered by her new charges, Lenora took to wearing sunglasses. She wore a floppy brimmed hat and tried to never look down. She thought that this approach might keep her from seeing hearts, but the hearts found her anyway. They followed her home on brisk walks around the block. They appeared in her bed when she pulled back the sheets. Lenora could not escape the hearts. Eventually she had thirteen in total. They bounced on her shoulders, they jumped at her ankles. Save for the original heart, which was content in its bowl of metallic, pink water and never gave Lenora any trouble, the twelve other hearts demanded everything of Lenora. And Lenora gave them everything she had. Why shouldn't she? The hearts loved her like she had never been loved.

*

Every night, before bed, Lenora sat on the floor. The hearts ran to her. They piled in her lap and beat their approval. Lenora was exhausted but validated. She sang to them. She read to them the sorts of things hearts liked hearing. Pablo Neruda, mostly. But also the personal ads.

"Divorced female, lapsed Catholic," Lenora would begin, and the hearts would flutter in her lap. "Seeks recovering priest for champagne and chess." If Lenora paused for too long between ads, the hearts would jump into the newspaper and rattle it. *More,* they seemed to say. *Go on! Go on!*

So, Lenora would. *Single man, gay and Jewish, seeks badminton partner. Married but lonely atheist seeks backseat hugs in secret parking lots. Adventurous couple seeks adventurous couple for naked skydiving. Hippie seeks hipster for road/acid trips.*

*

One night, when Lenora had read her heart out and the hearts were asleep, thumping contentedly in her lap, she came across a personal ad like no other. *Single woman completely unsure of how to love or be loved,* it read. *But completely sure she is ready to try.*

Lenora couldn't sleep that night. She kept the personal ad folded in a square in her pocket, for a week. She bathed the hearts and read them Neruda and let them take from her what they needed to take. But she did not read them the ad. When she finally decided to call the number, she did so in the car, locked inside, while the hearts hammered the hood and windshield like heavy rain.

"Hello," Lenora said, when the voicemail picked up. "Ready To Try? This is Also Ready To Try." The two hearts that Lenora had found on her stoop in the fresh seafood box pounded on the glass. Lenora thought they might explode. "I was wondering," she said to the voicemail, "if you might like to meet."

Ready To Try did. Later that day, Lenora received a thumbs-up emoji on her phone and a *7PM?* And Lenora responded with her own thumbs-up and her address, before considering what she was going to do with the hearts. She needed a plan, and fast.

Lenora put on a long prairie skirt. She located her copy of Shakespeare's sonnets. She ran around the house, the hearts at her heels, until they were exhausted. Then she sat on the floor and called them to her lap. She read 89 of the 154 sonnets until, finally, all the hearts were asleep. Gingerly, Lenora lifted her skirt full of hearts and closed the front of it with her fist. She stepped out of the skirt and walked in her underwear to the metal garbage can in the garage. She knotted the skirt and set the hearts down in the can. She noiselessly placed the lid on the can. She put two bricks on the lid. Then she put on a new, fresh skirt and lipstick and waited.

At seven, Ready knocked on Lenora's door. Lenora took a deep breath and looked through the peephole. Ready looked exactly that. Her eyes were both hopeful and nervous. She shifted her weight from one foot to the other. Lenora envisioned her heart as plum-colored and muscular from longing. Lenora put her hand on the knob, and then she removed it. She put it back on the knob and took a breath. When Ready knocked a second time, Lenora opened the door and smiled.

"Hello," she said.

Ready held out her hand. "Hello," she said back.

Behind Lenora, past the kitchen, past the hallway that connected to the attached garage, Lenora heard a single metallic thump. And then she heard another. She gave an awkward smile and cleared her throat. The hearts were waking up, it seemed, and before Lenora could invite Ready inside, the hearts launched into a distant, rhythmic banging.

"What's that?" Ready asked.

"Oh." Lenora shrugged, walking out onto the stoop and closing the door behind her. "I have some shoes in the dryer."

*

Lenora and Ready went out to dinner. They ate roast beef and talked about all the things they weren't, all the things they'd never done, all the things they would probably never end up being. When they were finished, they went for a long walk. Lenora was afraid she might find another heart, or that another heart would find her, so she refused to look down. Instead, she looked right at Ready and Ready looked right at her. At the end of the night, on their way back to Lenora's, Lenora worried about asking Ready in. Not because she wasn't ready for Ready, but because of the hearts. How would Lenora explain the shoes still in the dryer?

"You'll have to excuse my house," Lenora said as they pulled in the driveway. "It's pretty messy."

The headlights from Ready's car shone right at the front door, right into the house. "It's also open," she said, pointing. "I think you've been robbed."

Lenora and Ready got out of the car. They approached the house warily. Inside the front door, Lenora turned on the foyer lights. She handed an umbrella to Ready for protection. She took another for herself.

"I don't see anything odd," Ready said.

Lenora looked around the front hall. She peered into the tiny living room, the tiny kitchen. Both were her-messy, but not thief-messy. "Excuse me," she said. "I need to check on those shoes. In the dryer."

Out in the garage, Lenora found the trash can toppled. The lid had rolled into a corner. The two bricks had broken in half. The prairie skirt was off to one side, wrinkled and unknotted. The hearts were nowhere to be found.

Lenora ran back into the house. She flew through the kitchen and the living room, past Ready and into the bedroom. On the floor was the fishbowl, shattered. On the rug, a circle of damp pink. Lenora got down on her knees and looked under the bed. She stood and tore back the sheets. She went to the dresser and pulled out its drawers. She felt something inside her break free and rise—a scream that came out and brought Ready to her.

"What is it?" Ready appeared in the bedroom doorway. "Tell me what's happening."

Lenora fell to her knees and put her face in her hands. "My heart," she said. "It's gone. It was right here when I left, but now it's gone."

Ready reached out a hand to Lenora. "Let me help you up."

Lenora shook her head. "You don't understand. All the other hearts did something to it. They stole it," she sobbed. "They took it. They took my one good heart away from me."

Lenora cried into her hands. She thought of the sacrifices she had made to the twelve demanding hearts. She thought of the first heart's selflessness, its unconditional nature.

"Wait here," Ready said.

Lenora looked up. She watched Ready leave. Eventually, Lenora went out into the living room and sat in the dark. Outside, she could see the beam of a flashlight bounce up and down. Ready was walking the yard in careful lines, down and back, left and right. Lenora went to the window and watched. She grew still and serene. After a while, something returned and settled inside her, like a heart dropped into a bowl. Lenora went to the open front door and stood. "Ready," she called out. "It's okay. You can stop. You don't have to look anymore."

Ready paused as if making sure she had heard Lenora right. Ready and Lenora both stood still and quiet. Finally, Lenora waved and Ready waved back. And then Ready turned off the flashlight and headed back to the house in the dark, her footsteps thumping, thumping, thumping to where Lenora stood waiting.

GOOD GUYS

T O BE FAIR, the kid was asking for it. The moment he
stumbled into Holbrook College's cooperative dorm with
his archaic set of yam-colored suitcases and big Midwestern
smile, he might as well have passed around engraved invitations
to his own ass-kicking. He arrived at the Collective during a rowdy
dinner of wine and lentil loaf, and as he stood grinning in the
dining room doorway, the late August sun made a nimbus of his
prairie-colored hair.

"Hello, folks!" he said, breathless with innocence. "I'm Leonard
Salts from Illinois. You can call me Leonard or Lee or Leo or Leon—
whatever floats your boat."

Leonard's earnestness was palpable. It brought all forty
Collectives—their banter and scraping of tin plates—to a hush.

"Looks like I got the last room on campus, but I figure that's
what happens when you can't make up your mind between New
Hampshire and Ohio." Leonard shook his head like he was an utter
fool. "Ohio, New Hampshire. New Hampshire, Ohio. Finally, I just
looked in the bathroom mirror and said to myself, 'Leonard, you nut!
You bona fide coconut! Ohio? You *know* Ohio. It's just like Illinois
but with less corn and more porn.'" The kid lowered his voice like

he was letting everyone in on a family secret. "At least that's what my dad, Walter Salts, says. I know, I know. Walter Salts, Walter Salts. My grandmother was a poet and she didn't even know it. Or maybe, just maybe, she did."

Leonard gave a little snort and addressed his suitcases. Two were tucked under his arms and two he held by their silver handles. Like a bellhop, he stacked them in a pile on the dining room floor from biggest to smallest. On top was a squat and square ladies' cosmetic case that the whole room seemed to consider at once. Leonard, unburdened, went on. "But, back to the why and how. In the end, New Hampshire picked me and I picked New Hampshire and the administration picked this place for me to live. Well, not picked actually, because it was the only room left. But here I am and nice to meet you all. Again: Leonard Salts from Ursula, Illinois. Probably never heard of it, but now you have and you can no longer say you haven't."

Leonard gave a little bow. There was a quiet chortle or two, followed by a low whistle from the rear of the room. It seemed for a moment that no one knew what to say. The Collectives in their designer love beads and imported leather sandals looked at one another, this way and that, as if they were being pranked and one of them was responsible. At long last, Teddy Yates, the Collective's president, stood and lifted his coffee mug of wine.

"Well, I say welcome!" Teddy's voice took on the showman's tone that his dorm mates had come to expect, a tone Leonard mistook as genuine. "The Collective is exactly that: a collection of all sorts and all types. I think you'll find yourself right at home here. In fact, ten minutes from now, I bet you the farm you won't miss Nebraska at all."

Leonard's smile fell a bit. He corrected Teddy with an "Illinois," but his state of origin went unheard in the roar of applause for Teddy. The next thing Leonard knew, he was being pushed down into a dining chair and up to a table where someone slid him a tin plate of lentil loaf and a full mug of wine. Leonard, in the chaos, tried to insist he could partake of neither—one because of his weak stomach, the other because of his morals—but the Collectives collectively pouted as if the whole bunch of them might burst into tears, and after much cheering and jeering, Leonard choked down what was in front of him before promptly regurgitating all of it back onto the table. The applause that followed was so deafening and lengthy, that Leonard, pale and clammy, eventually gave a weak smile in spite of himself. Then Teddy yanked him up by the armpits and clapped him on the back and showed him to his third-floor room.

"Welcome home, Nebraska," Teddy said, gesturing at the concrete walls and iron bed. "You're not in Kansas anymore."

Leonard opened his mouth and closed it. "Right," he said meekly. "Thanks."

*

Teddy wasn't sure why he started in on Leonard, but he felt compelled to. When he woke the next day and saw Leonard sitting in the dining room with a tall glass of milk, he recalled a horse he'd once seen broken. Teddy's sister had once been into the equestrian world out on Long Island, and one summer Teddy had tagged along to see how people went about training a show horse. A woman had put a rust-colored horse with flared nostrils on a long leash and trotted it in a circle for a good hour. First clockwise and then counterclockwise. The woman explained to Teddy and his sister that she held a whip, just in case, but she rarely needed to use it. She maintained that repetition was stronger than violence, and Teddy remembered this as he watched Leonard take a long pull from his milk and forget to wipe his upper lip. Teddy could see it clearly; the world would devour Leonard if someone didn't show him the ropes, so Teddy decided that a few times a day, he'd take it upon himself to get out the ropes and dangle them in front of Leonard's angelic corn-fed face. Never mind if this behavior wasn't in keeping with the Collective's original mission of love and let love, live and let live. It was for Leonard's own good.

*

For the first week or so, it was just "Nebraska" whenever Teddy saw Leonard. "Missing Nebraska?" he might say, or: "This is my new buddy Leonard. He's from Nebraska."

Leonard would always reply smiling. "Well . . . actually. It's Illinois. Ursula, Illinois." To which Teddy would give his head a big oafish shake or tap his temple and say: "Geez! Silly me! That's right! Illinois!" only to repeat the "Nebraska" trick a few hours later. When, after about ten days, Leonard quit smiling and quit correcting Teddy about Nebraska, Teddy made fast to rewin Leonard's affection so the training could continue. "Hey, Peoria!" Teddy took up saying. "My man! Peoria!" This new nickname seemed to equally confuse and appease Leonard, and once Teddy felt Leonard was less skittish, he ramped it up with unpredictable shout-outs: "Hey, Tin Man!" across campus. "Hey, Dorothy!" across the dining hall. "Hey, Ozzie, my friend. Ozzie Oz!" down the hall.

Within a month, Leonard looked tired. But also less naive. Teddy gave himself credit for this ripening, but something about it nagged him, too. What it was, he couldn't explain. There was just a general unease about what he'd taken upon himself to do. Teddy sensed he either needed to call it quits or double down to make himself feel better. And one night, at odds with himself, he wandered up to Leonard's room to get an idea of how he needed to proceed.

"Nebraska," he heard himself say unexpectedly as he knocked on Leonard's door. "It's your biggest fan. Teddy."

There was a long pause and then Teddy heard a quiet "Come in."

Teddy opened the door slowly and took a peek inside. Then he threw the door open wide in awe. "Holy shit!" Teddy said. "This is some setup you've got here."

Leonard looked up at Teddy from his desk. He wore magnifying spectacles and had been tinkering with something miniscule. His eyes grew bigger than big at Teddy's praise. "You think so, Teddy?"

Teddy wandered around the room with his arms crossed in front of him while he inspected Leonard's displays. "So I think, Leonard. So I think."

Leonard's room was nothing short of a museum, a war museum to be exact, but which war exactly was lost on Teddy, who knew little about history other than his own personal one. "What is all this stuff?" he asked. "How'd you fit all this into your suitcases?"

"Revolutionary War replicas," Leonard said. "Uniforms, bullets, buttons, and the like." Leonard smiled, quickly regaining his day-one enthusiasm and speed. "My mother's been mailing it to me. I make everything to be as authentic as possible. I'm a faker-maker, you could say. Nothing I create is the real thing, but it passes as such all the time."

Teddy smiled. "So, you scam people?"

Leonard took off his spectacles and set down his tools. "Of course not!" he said. "Absolutely, resolutely not. I make things for myself and occasionally museums." He stood up from his desk and dug through a stack of photographs. "I had one museum request a pair of colonial boots and, by Jove, I made them a pair of colonial boots. See? Here you are." He held up a photograph in front of Teddy's face. The boots in question looked like a pair of women's old shoes. "You can't tell the difference between these and George Washington's. I ran over them with my father's John Deere to break them in, and then I oiled them and ran over them, oiled them and ran over them, and then finally packed them in some dirt for a week until . . . abracadabra! Museum quality." Leonard beamed like he had on the first night, before the lentil loaf and wine had gotten the best of him. "My grandmother thinks I crossed the Delaware in a past life. I've been eat up with this stuff since I was three." Leonard went to the yam-colored cosmetic case and brought it to Teddy. "Open it," he said.

Teddy looked at Leonard's ecstatic face. The horse was completely off its lead now. Teddy was going to have to start from scratch. "Go on," Leonard urged. "Look inside."

Inside the case was a velvet box about the size of a sandwich, and inside of that was what appeared to be dentures. "They're Washington's teeth," Leonard gushed. "Well, a replica of. They took me a year to make. I made them out of pork ribs. Well, pork rib bones."

Leonard was on cloud nine. Teddy thought for a moment of how he might be able to knock him down to cloud two or three. He closed the velvet box and put it back into the case and gave a long, drawn-out sigh. "You know, Peoria, the Collective was founded during the Vietnam War." Teddy handed the cosmetic case back to Leonard, who seemed to wilt a little. "Thirty years ago, some honest-to-goodness flower children got together on this campus in the name of peace and petitioned for their own cooperative dormitory." Teddy looked for a place to sit, but finding none, went and leaned against Leonard's desk, knocking several small tools to the floor in the process. "These were peaceable student-activists who wanted to live in harmony... cook together, bang on some tambourines, stand up to injustice. They didn't believe in Wall Street or mousetraps or razors. And they sure as shit didn't believe in war."

Leonard went from looking discouraged to scared. "Oh, I'm as peaceful as they get, Teddy. I'm just into the history of it all. That's all. Really."

Teddy leaned up from the desk and more tools fell to the floor. He knew good and well that the present-day Collective was more drugs than hugs, a gathering of imposters—young men and women who hailed from money but dressed as if they didn't. Potheads with no political agenda who ate beans for show, but prime rib when they went home to their parents' country houses.

"*I* believe you, Leonard," Teddy said, positioning himself as Leonard's one and only confidante. "But the others wouldn't." Teddy took a final stroll around the room with his arms crossed, as if now assessing a police lineup. "We'll keep this just between the two of us, okay?"

Leonard nodded silently and Teddy let himself out. Alone in the stairwell, Teddy paused between the third and second floors. He could hear his own heart pounding. He knew he was terrible. He knew he was being just plain rotten. He didn't know why he'd ever started in on Leonard in the first place. He'd never acted like this in his entire life, at least not that he could recall. On some occasions, maybe he had been a little arrogant, but this behavior was just above and beyond, and Teddy knew it. Far off, from some Collective dorm room, Teddy could hear a whoop of laughter and bongo drums. *What a charade,* some voice inside his head said. *A never-ending costume party.* Teddy's stomach gave a little flip. Maybe he could lay off a little. Maybe he could give the horse a vacation from training, let it out to graze.

Teddy went down to his dorm room and lit what was left of a joint. He pinched it between his fingers like a dead, white moth and turned off the lights. He lay down on his futon and let himself remember Leonard in the doorway the first night. How his amber hair lit up like a halo. How he stacked his luggage like a child stacked building blocks. Teddy let himself feel guilty about everything for a while. He even went so far as to say a prayer, which was something he hadn't done since he was maybe seven, when he'd wished to God that his parents would stay together, which they hadn't. *Please let Leonard like me,* the prayer went. *Please let Leonard think I'm a good guy.* Teddy repeated the prayer again and again until he felt certain his prayer would be answered. After a while, he fell asleep peacefully and without remorse.

*

Teddy did the best he could to ride Leonard less hard. He stuck with "Peoria" and "Ozzie" and dropped "Nebraska" and "Dorothy." A few times a week, he went by Leonard's room to watch him work. He'd sit on the bed and Leonard would sit at his desk, and for a while, Leonard would talk about Illinois, the family farm, the cow he'd raised that won a trophy, the way his mother made three-day beans. Sometimes he amused Teddy with rural tales he swore were true, like how he'd trained a cat to nurse a litter of possums or how a tornado had once corked their chimney with a live goat. One day, however, he really set Teddy's head spinning with the casual announcement that his maternal grandfather was a full-blood Shawnee.

Teddy snorted. "Please. I refuse to go on believing your 4-H bullshit."

Leonard kept at work at his desk, intent and scraping. "It's true blue," he said calmly. "I'm related to Tecumseh. He's my great-times-five-grandfather. Great, great, great, great, great."

Teddy sat up on Leonard's bed and stared. "Stop yanking my chain," he said. "What sort of Tecumseh grandkid sits around on his blond ass making Revolutionary War collectibles?"

Leonard scraped and scraped. "No man is without conflict," he said. "That's what Walter Salts always says." Leonard turned around and gave Teddy a big, mid-American grin. "You should try to get into the enemy's shoes some time. To see things from the other side." Leonard turned back to his work. "My father says if you don't fight the war on the inside, you'll fight it on the outside."

Teddy didn't know what to say. Leonard suddenly struck him as complicated. If Leonard was telling the truth, he was a hypocrite. If he was lying, then he was everything Teddy had never imagined he could be. Teddy sat and stared at the back of Leonard's twenty-four-karat head until he could name the feeling he felt. *Impressed.* Leonard turned as silent as a monk, and Teddy sat in admiration until the whole room went golden and time stopped and the two of them were suspended in amber. Teddy watched until all he could see was a column of light. Until all he could hear were the soft sounds of industry. The next thing Teddy knew, he was waking, blissful, in Leonard's bed. Leonard stood smiling at the bedside looking down at Teddy. In one hand, Leonard held his scraping tool. The other hand, empty, reached out slow and tender to brush Teddy's cheek.

"You fell asleep," Leonard laughed gently. "Right on my bed like a big ole teddy bear."

Teddy's face burned where Leonard had touched it. Teddy put his own palm to his cheek and sat up, overcome with a sudden, inexplicable sorrow that he quickly replaced with anger. "I have to go," he said, his palm still on his cheek. "You shouldn't have let me stay so long." Then Teddy rose and left without another word.

*

After that, Teddy didn't go back to Leonard's room. In fact, he avoided him altogether for a good while out of fear. Then one October morning, Teddy saw Leonard alone at breakfast. Leonard looked lost and vulnerable, like he had the first day, and Teddy joined him at the table despite himself.

"Making any boots?" Teddy asked. "Any pork rib dentures?"

Leonard lit up like a harvest moon and set down his milk. His upper lip was foamy. His eyes were bright. It seemed to Teddy he had grown more pure and perfect in his absence. "Why, yes I am, thank you for asking," Leonard said. "My great uncle wants a set of Washington teeth. He knows a fellow who knows a fellow who knows someone who works at a famous history museum, which is actually located right here. Well, not here in New Hampshire, but here in the United States. Massachusetts, maybe." Leonard leaned forward confidentially. "This could be a big break for me, Teddy. I mean, I'd still go to school here and get my history degree, but I'd have something waiting for me when I got out." Leonard looked as if he might cry from joy and Teddy's stomach did the same somersault it had the night he'd resorted to prayer. "Don't say anything, promise? I know you won't. You're the best friend I've got here and I trust you." Then Leonard reached out and touched Teddy's hand on top of the table and answered a prayer. "You're a good guy, Teddy."

Teddy felt his hand go hot and his brain go cold. He shot up from the table with such force his tin plate clattered to the floor. "Don't do that," Teddy commanded. "Not ever."

With that, Teddy ran from the Collective and out to the

campus's far field. When he made it halfway across, he stood in
the damp morning grass and leaned over with his hands on his
knees and was sick. He stayed that way for some time, fearing
he might collapse if he straightened his spine. Bent over, Teddy
fought against something inside himself that he couldn't name and
was sick again. Maybe the problem was that the horse hadn't been
trained at all. Maybe Teddy had let it out to pasture before it had
learned a single thing. Teddy remembered the woman and the show
horse. He remembered her whip, rare but ready. He wondered what
kind of horse she had ever had to use it on. Maybe it wasn't on one
that was too wild, but on one that was too mild. Teddy spit into the
grass and put his hands on his hips. He decided that was the case. If
he didn't act fast, Leonard would wither before Thanksgiving. Teddy
frowned for a long time at a span of yellow maples. When he had
come up with a good plan, he went on to class empty-handed so he
wouldn't have to go back and chance Leonard.

*

Teddy's original plan was to feed Leonard a few pot brownies in
the common room. A gathering of Collectives would put on some
Pink Floyd, pass around a plate of cosmic fudge, and the next thing
everyone knew, Leonard would break free of his cornhusk. It would
be like attending the birth of a baby. Everyone Teddy ran the idea
past thought it was the greatest undertaking the Collective could
ever attempt. But then things got out of control. Teddy made the
mistake of mentioning Leonard's war hobbies. He made the mistake of mentioning the Washington teeth and Tecumseh and the
goat in the chimney and the colonial boots. He made the mistake
of picking Leonard's dorm room lock while Leonard was at class
and taking a bunch of Collectives on a tour of Leonard's collectibles.

They tried on his wigs. They tried on his tricornered hat. They laughed and laughed until they had a better idea than pot brownies in the common room.

"A tea party," someone suggested.

"Like a Boston one," someone countered.

At that point, Teddy knew it was beyond him. But having it beyond him relieved him of responsibility, so Teddy gave his blessing. An enthusiastic one.

"Your only job is to get him there," Howie Ames said.

"Dressed as George Washington," Gavin Thomas said.

*

Leonard wasn't too keen on going in uniform after what Teddy had told him about the original flower children, but after a few brownies, Leonard didn't know Illinois from Nebraska.

"You look great, Peoria," Teddy said, as he buttoned Leonard's waistcoat. "More all-American than ever."

Leonard didn't respond. His eyes were big and black, as empty as a shark's. Teddy equipped Leonard with a cardboard musket and straightened his wig and the two presidents went out to the far field where a bonfire the size of a teepee raged.

"They're coming!" someone shouted, when they saw Teddy and Leonard approaching.

"Who's coming?" a chorus asked.

"The British!" another chorus answered. "The British! The British are coming!"

Though incorrect, Teddy found this hilarious, but Leonard, in the flickering, distant glow, stopped in terror.

"Come on, Peoria," Teddy said. "The party can't go on without you."

And that was when Leonard took off, fast and frantic. He had an unexpected agility, and Teddy thought, with some level of parental admiration, that maybe he had, once again, underestimated him. Maybe he knew nothing about him at all. He watched with awe and horror as Leonard made for the dark span of distant maples, where the far field met the wilderness. The Collectives, beyond inebriated, were delighted by this unexpected turn.

"Go, Nebraska, go!" someone hooted.

"All the way to Mount Vernon!" another shouted.

In the glow of the bonfire, all that Teddy could make out as he tried to follow Leonard's retreat was the white wig bouncing in the night, growing smaller and smaller against the jagged silhouette of the forest like the terrified end of a cottontail. There was a chorus of laughter that followed when the wig could no longer be seen. It was laughter that soon faded to an intoxicated murmuring and later to a glazed glee of stupidity.

When the sun came up a few hours later, innocent over the woods, no one seemed to recall what had happened—to Leonard or themselves. The fire was now nothing but a handful of ashes. The discarded baking pans and tambourines dotted the scene like battle shields. The Collectives eventually rose up from beneath their dewy blankets and squinted out empty at the world, before staggering back into the dormitory for eggs and sleep.

Teddy's fear unfolded with the day. At first his anxiety was manageable. He stayed out in the far field for the morning, picking up debris, pouring warm beer in the ashes, staring off at the maples in the hopes he'd soon see Leonard emerge, rumpled but golden, shaking his head in good humor, holding his flattened wig in one hand and waving *Hello! Here I am, Teddy!* with the other. But by noon, there was no sign of Leonard, neither in the Collective nor in the field, so Teddy went off into the woods on his own. He kept reminding himself of Leonard's unexpected agility as he walked. He reminded himself that Leonard had grown up on a farm and had raised a cow from calf to bull. Teddy tried to imagine Leonard strolling over fallen trees and whistling with the birds, but instead he saw him pale and dead on a bed of crimson leaves. He tried to imagine Leonard sitting on a stump in his Revolutionary garb, buttoning his boots and reciting the Preamble, but again, Teddy saw him dead and white, his eyes open in a last moment of panic that Teddy had orchestrated.

Teddy came back from the woods in the late afternoon. By the time the sun began its descent, Leonard still had not returned and Teddy was near panic. He called a meeting of all the Collectives, but some were in too poor a shape from the night before to attend, and of those who did, nearly half of them found Leonard's absence insignificant.

"Nebraska's fine," Gavin said. "Schoolchildren have eaten worse brownies."

"He's probably in town," Howie said. "Have you even checked the diner? Twenty bucks he's there right now drinking a six-pack of milk."

Teddy gnawed his bottom lip. "I think we should tell the administration. Maybe campus security."

There were some audible groans and Gavin shook his head. "Leave the school out of it. The kid'll turn up eventually. Dapper and dumb as ever."

The meeting adjourned without Teddy's blessing. Teddy went up to Leonard's room to see if he had crept back into the Collective when no one was watching. But Leonard wasn't there. Teddy sat at Leonard's desk and turned on the desk lamp. He tried on Leonard's magnifying glasses. He scraped at a brass button with a dental tool. Then he took off the glasses and curled up on Leonard's bed and prayed the prayer he'd prayed before, plus one more. *Please let Leonard like me. Please let Leonard think I'm a good guy. Please let Leonard be alive.*

*

Three days later and three towns over, Leonard was eventually found. He wasn't dead, but he was dehydrated and weak and had a broken arm. The Collective gathered around the common room television to watch the local news. Leonard was still dressed as a soldier. He still had on his old wig, as well as a new cast, as two policemen helped him into a cruiser.

"Look at him!" Gavin said. "He's as white as a sheet."

"Check out his eyes." Howie whistled. "They don't look real."

Teddy hung back in the common room and stared at the floor while the newscaster gave his report. Leonard had been found on an elderly couple's front porch. When confronted, he'd told authorities he was the first president of the United States and that he was originally from Nebraska. Thanks to a student ID, the cops were able to determine that his name was Leonard Salts and he was from Ursula, Illinois. He was now in good hands and being sent back to his parents, accompanied by a school counselor. "He's a lucky young man," the newscaster said in closing. "He was pretty bad off when he was found."

The Collectives, save for Teddy, clapped when the segment cut to a commercial.

"All's well that ends well," one said.

"Talk about making history," said another.

*

Teddy skipped class for the rest of the week. On Saturday, a tall sad man, accompanied by a dean of some sort, came to pack up Leonard's things. Teddy stood in the hall and listened while they wrapped Leonard's creations in newspaper.

"I can't figure out what went wrong," the tall man said. "Leonard always had a good head on his shoulders."

There was a long silence. Teddy's stomach spun one way and then another.

"Some people do better close to home," the administrator finally said. "I'm sure he'll bounce right back once he gets back to what he knows."

Teddy left the hallway and went to his room. An hour later, he watched from his window as the tall man and the dean walked from the Collective with the yam-colored suitcases and a dolly full of cardboard boxes. Teddy watched until they disappeared around a wooded bend in campus. He watched the bend until the sky was black. Teddy couldn't stop thinking about Leonard or the teeth in the velvet box. He couldn't stop thinking about the museum waiting for the teeth, and how they might never receive their order and Leonard would lose his chance. But mostly he thought about watching Leonard work—his bent back and the gentle scrape of his tools and the slow evenings suspended in amber.

Teddy sank into a deep depression. Within a week, he took a leave of absence and went home to his mother in Massachusetts. She babied him with soup. She gave him half of her Prozac prescription. Teddy spent his time sleeping and reading old comic books and trying not to think about Leonard. On Thanksgiving, Teddy picked up the phone and called Information and got a number for a Walter Salts in Ursula, but before he could convince himself to call, he burned the piece of paper the number was on. He lit a match and held it to the paper and dropped the paper right before it burned his fingers. The ashes of Walter Salts's number left a little brown scar on Teddy's white bedspread.

"Why don't you go somewhere after the holidays?" his mother suggested. "Somewhere where people really have it bad? A place that will make you feel better about yourself?"

Teddy was doubtful, but he took her advice. In January, he went somewhere hot and humid and primitive—a place where he was tall and godly and the bearer of good and necessary things. It turned out his mother was right: seeing people worse off than himself really did put Teddy in a better mood. Before long, his spirits soared. He saw himself as a benevolent king. One who was good with a shovel, a soup ladle, a campfire guitar. Teddy gained approval, mostly from himself; he grew nearly giddy with self-righteousness. By the time he returned to the States that summer, Teddy had, for all intents and purposes, erased Leonard Salts from his memory.

*

Years later on a Sunday drive home from the beach, Teddy stopped at a rest area with his young family. It was a dark and dated pit stop, but it had clean-enough bathrooms, and while Teddy's wife tended to their son and daughter, Teddy stood in the vestibule with his hands on his hips and stared at the vending machines. He peered into one that offered crackers and chips, and then into a second that offered water and juice, before he finally paused to consider the space between the two machines. There, tucked in the shadows and bolted to the wall, was a small, nondescript box. Curious, Teddy moved closer and saw that the box was made of glass and steel. It was smudged with fingerprints but inside were a set of yellowed false teeth and three brass buttons and a neat row of crude bullets. Teddy frowned. He felt his stomach do a little flip, and he leaned in closer still. There wasn't a plaque anywhere to be found, just a little strip of paper inside the box, upon which was typed the word: REPLICAS. Teddy bent over until his nose touched the box. He stared until his eyes watered. For a moment, he could hear the scraping of Leonard's tools and was back on Leonard's bed, suspended in amber, right at the threshold of the afterlife. He saw Leonard's nimbus of hair, felt Leonard's warm hand on his cheek. He heard Leonard say: *You're the best friend that I've got here, Teddy. You're a good guy.*

And then: his wife and children. Loud and soapy and fresh, their shoes squeaking against the floor. "Vending machines!" they squealed. "Can we have quarters, Daddy? Can we? Can we?"

Teddy couldn't speak. Their presence was suddenly tin plates clattering all around. He stormed from the rest area and went out to the car and sat panting behind the wheel. When his wife and children finally climbed back in, Teddy started the car and gunned the engine. He put all the windows down and drove off, fast and erratically, first in one lane and then in another. In the roar of the hot summer wind, as he sped westward, Teddy could once again see the horse. It had gone mad from fear and was galloping toward the horizon in a cloud of dust. Behind it, clinging to the training lead, was Teddy. He thought he had let go long ago, but he realized he never had. He realized he never could, even if he wanted to.

THE HORSE LAMP

J ARROD HAD BEEN called to the girl's house to fix her
satellite dish, but when he got to the peeling blue rental and
walked around its weedy perimeter, he saw that the girl didn't
have a satellite dish. She had cable. Jarrod tried to explain the difference between the two services while the girl stood barefoot on
the stoop wearing a see-through tank top and a pair of minuscule
cutoffs. Jarrod noticed that the girl had dirty feet—filthy, really—
and that her toenails were painted the color of mustard. Both of her
pinkie toes were curled in for warmth against the other toes like
two cold grubs. While Jarrod talked, he imagined the girl shoeless
at the drugstore, standing in the nail polish aisle for a while before
stealing a bottle of yellow polish when no one was looking. He saw
the girl walk right past the cashier, carefree and careless, her brown
feet slapping the tile. For a good portion of his satellite-and-cable
explanation, Jarrod looked at the girl's feet and imagined her shop-
lifting. He did this to avoid looking her in the eye. Every time he
looked up, there the girl was, staring at him hard and brave and
dumb, chewing slow on a wad of gum. It made Jarrod feel dizzy to
look at her head-on. It made him feel like he might keel over in
the red landscape gravel that was scattered around the tiny house.

"What I'm getting at," Jarrod finally said, "is that I can't fix your satellite dish, because you got no satellite dish. And I'm not allowed to fix the cable seeing how I don't even work for the cable company."

The girl twisted a lock of dry copper hair around one of her fingers until her finger turned lilac. "Aw, now," she said. "Ain't fixing a TV just fixing a TV? Whatever happened to being a gentleman?" She winked at Jarrod and switched her wad of gum from one cheek to the other. Jarrod could see her flat breasts through the white tank top. They looked like two eggs in a skillet and he thought he might lose consciousness. "I'm sure you can figure out how to fix it." The girl exhaled. "I really need my TV because TV is my whole life."

Jarrod looked over his shoulder. He looked at the white company van parked on the street. There was a picture of a big red satellite painted on the van. The driver's side window was half-down but it didn't look like it was going to rain. "All right," Jarrod said. "But real quick or else I might get fired."

Inside the rental house, a giant dog with clouded eyes got itself up on all fours with some struggle when Jarrod entered. It came over to Jarrod and nosed around his crotch and thumped its heavy tail against the wall in apparent approval.

"Get the fuck off the nice man, Oreo," the girl said. "Don't worry about Oreo. He's my stupid roommate's stupid dog. He doesn't bite or nothing. He just bothers the living shit out of everyone." The girl kicked laundry and magazines out of the way with a dirty foot. "You want something to drink?" she asked. "I got the blue Gatorade. The light blue kind. And I got tap water and milk, but I don't think the milk's any good anymore."

When the girl bent over to push some old newspapers out of their path, Jarrod could see high up where the girl's legs changed from legs to ass. Her skin went from smooth and tan to white and dimpled. There was nothing gradual about it. It was like two countries on top of each other, ice cream on a cone. "I'm not thirsty," Jarrod said. "But you better show me that TV. I can't take all day here."

"All right," the girl said. "But it ain't much."

The girl took Jarrod down a banged-up narrow hall. She opened a door at the end of it and a burst of air-conditioned air hit Jarrod in the face. The room was as dark as midnight and it smelled like fruit punch. The girl clicked on a little lamp and the little lamp flickered on to reveal a mattress on the floor covered in clothes. The walls were sloppy-painted the color of bubblegum. In the corner, an outdated television sat on a milk crate, its rabbit-ear antennae wrapped in aluminum foil.

"I'm a mess," the girl said. "Always will be."

Jarrod waded through towels and clothes. He went to the television and held one of the antennae ears in his hand. "You have cable and you don't even have this hooked up to cable," he said. "This thing is just plugged into the wall like a radio."

The girl gave a sheepish smile and shrugged. "Aw, all right," she said. "I'm busted."

Jarrod let go of the antennae and scowled.

"See, now. I didn't call for no repairman," the girl said. "I'm just laying an egg is all."

Jarrod looked at the girl the way she'd looked at him when he had tried to explain the difference between satellite and cable.

"Ovulation," the girl said. "This is that week in the month I'm most likely to get pregnant and I need someone to get me pregnant."

"Ohhh no," Jarrod said, suddenly enlightened. He went to step over the clothes, to go back the way he'd come, but Oreo was standing right in the way he needed to go, slapping his big tail against a dresser missing most of its drawers. "I ain't getting anybody pregnant. No ma'am, no sir."

The girl backed up against her bedroom door and by the time Jarrod got to her, she had her spine pressed up against the doorknob. "The Robinsons' baby," she said fast. "I let it drown in the ocean." Jarrod went to reach behind the girl and she lifted up a knee. "I was their babysitter last summer and I let go of the baby and it drowned." The girl choked for a second, like she might cry. "They never found it neither. Thanks to me, their baby wasn't only killed but lost, too." Jarrod looked at the girl's raised knee. He didn't think she could do him much harm. "They're pretty bad off now, the Robinsons are. Who wouldn't be with a baby at the bottom of the ocean? But I'm going to get pregnant and have them a baby and put the baby on their porch in a laundry basket and then leave town for good."

Jarrod put one hand on the girl's knee and reached behind her with his other for the doorknob. He'd get rough with her if he had to. He thought about how he could move her. He could shove her to the side and run. He could push her to the floor. He could do that and get free and back to the van, but before Jarrod could decide exactly how, the girl reached out and clicked off the little lamp and the room went midnight again. Jarrod felt the girl's hands, cold and gentle, one on his knee and one on his forearm. "Don't worry," she said softly. "I don't have anything you can catch. I just got me a fresh egg and it's not going to stay fresh long."

The girl took Jarrod's hand and slid it up the back of her shorts' leg where the two countries met and before he knew it, Jarrod was doing what he hadn't planned on doing. He was stumbling with her over the sea of laundry, over to the mattress on the floor. Once they were down, the girl's tank top went off and Jarrod's hands were on her flat skillet chest. The room was cold and the girl was cold, so Jarrod put as much of himself onto her and into her as he could. The girl made little mouse-like squeaks. Jarrod heard himself breathe like he was being chased. He felt himself leave his body and come back into it, leave his body and come back into it. Up close, the girl smelled like cherries, and with his eyes closed, Jarrod couldn't help but imagine that all that was in him was going into the girl to make something that would solve a terrible problem.

When it was over, Jarrod opened his eyes and the girl clicked on another little lamp by the mattress on the floor. This lamp was shaped like a horse and where the lamp part rose out of the horse, right where a saddle might be, Jarrod imagined himself on the horse's back and the girl behind him, her arms around his waist. He suddenly saw himself as important. On the other side of the mattress, the girl stayed on her back and brought her knees to her chest.

"This keeps the swimmers in," she said matter-of-factly. "It gives them a chance to find the egg."

Jarrod noticed that the girl's top two teeth were crooked and as she concentrated on her position, they poked out over her bottom lip. For a second, Jarrod wanted to touch her face, gentle, but then a bolt of fear shot through him and he squeezed his eyes together.

"You need to come back tomorrow," she said. "We should do what we just did for at least five days in a row." Jarrod didn't know what to say to that. He felt again as if he might faint. He opened his eyes forcefully and got up from the mattress and put on his pants. He felt weak, like the time he'd had the flu as a boy. Like the time he'd given blood in high school. "You hear me?" the girl said. "Five more days."

Jarrod didn't answer. He went down the narrow hall and out to the van. Outside, the world was hot and blinding and he could

hardly breathe. When he sat down behind the wheel, he could see a
faint yellow dust all over the dashboard where the pollen had settled
while he and the girl had been in the dark, doing what they'd done.

*

Jarrod made a promise to himself that he wouldn't go back to the
girl. He spent the whole next day on roofs, adjusting satellites for
better reception. He explained to housewives and shut-ins and
blank, unemployed men how warm weather affected the satellites.
He told them how when roofs got hot, the pads that the satellites
sat on got soft. How the satellites shifted on the shingles and quit
working the way they were meant to work. He spent the day listening to himself talk to people who didn't care what he said, while he
heard, in a far corner of his mind, the girl, squeaking like a mouse.
Every so often, Jarrod could smell the smell of fruit punch in his
nose. He'd just be sitting on a roof, sweating and thinking of the
girl's cold, dark room when all of sudden it was cherries, everywhere.
It happened enough that by the time Jarrod got off work at six he
couldn't think straight. He couldn't think of anything to do other
than what he had promised himself he wouldn't.

"You been swimming?" the girl asked when he showed up on the
stoop. Her feet were still filthy, but this time her toes were painted the
color of the sky. She had on the same shorts, it seemed, but another
thin tank top, this one striped, that put her small breasts in jail.

"Might as well been," Jarrod said. "The roofs out there are hot."

"I imagine," the girl said like she wasn't imagining it at all. "Well,
come on in. I was about to give up on you."

Jarrod followed the girl inside the house and, on cue, the big
dog with the cloudy eyes got up with some struggle and came over to
Jarrod and nosed his crotch and thumped his tail against the wall.

"Oreo likes you more than he likes my roommate," the girl said, kicking more things out of the way with her filthy feet. "Dogs can smell liars, you know. And that's what his owner is—a big fat one."

Jarrod kept quiet and followed the girl down the narrow hall. When she opened her bedroom door and the darkness and coldness and smell of fruit punch washed over him like a wave, Jarrod felt relieved. There was some part of him that had been afraid it would be different than the day before, but it was like a tape rewound and played again—a song he was starting to know the words to. Inside, the girl clicked on the first lamp on the dresser and Jarrod saw the TV wrapped in foil and the sloppy pink walls.

"Still a mess," the girl said without apology. "Always will be." Then she clicked off the first lamp and took Jarrod by the hand and led him over to the mattress and down they went as they had before. In the cold dark, the girl made the same noises as before and Jarrod breathed like he was being chased and when it was all over, the girl clicked on the little horse lamp by the mattress and brought her knees to her chest and poked her two crooked front teeth out over her bottom lip. After some time, she spoke.

"I'm gonna tell you something I never told anyone before, but I didn't drop the Robinsons' baby on accident. I let go of her on purpose."

Jarrod squeezed his eyes shut until the black behind his eyes turned to violet. In his mind, he saw the horse from the horse lamp. He saw himself and the girl on the shiny orange horse and the girl's arms were wrapped around his waist. Behind his tight eyes, he and the girl were riding under a white sky across a desert of white sand. The girl was pregnant. A baby—their baby—grew inside her and pushed against Jarrod's back.

"I was just out there waist-deep in the ocean with the baby and

I was holding her under the armpits and dipping her down into the water. And every time I went and dipped her down in the cold water, the baby's face got all big and scared." The girl paused to make a sound, and Jarrod guessed she was imitating the baby's expression. "The way that baby made her face look just did something to me. It made me not like her. She just had this perfect world lined up for herself with her perfect mother and her perfect father and that face of hers just made me feel like the worst thing she was ever gonna know was cold water." The girl sighed. "I didn't like that. I knew she would grow up to be no good to anybody if her only trouble was cold water. So, I let go of her for a minute to see what would happen and she got away from me fast. The wave came and I let go and then she was gone."

The girl didn't say anything for a while. In Jarrod's mind, the horse galloped across the white sand noiselessly and without effort. The desert was neither hot nor cold and the more Jarrod rode the horse toward the horizon, it occurred to him that they weren't in the desert at all. They were at the bottom of the ocean—a drained one.

"The worst was when I had to turn around from where I was at to face the baby's parents back on the beach. I just turned and held up my empty hands and before long the helicopters came and the lifeguards came and everybody lined up on the beach waiting like the queen was coming in on a boat." The girl let a little whistle escape through her crooked teeth. "The baby's mother was something else. She turned into a monster right then and there in front of everyone. She crawled back and forth on the sand like a dog. She even foamed at the mouth."

The orange horse slowed to a trot and Jarrod got off and the girl stayed on and Jarrod grabbed the horse's reins and brought the horse to a walk. He led the horse to a long, white dune, and at the top of it Jarrod and the girl looked out over the seafloor. There were bleached white skeletal shipwrecks and biplanes, there were white arching temple bones of blue whales, there were giant white conch shells and lost white shipping containers, tipped on their sides to spill white, flaking rubbish. There were old fishing masts like fossilized spines and anchors made of talc and off to the side there was the baby—a white plaster garden cherub covered in barnacles. Jarrod pointed to it and the girl nodded and Jarrod walked the horse out to the baby. When Jarrod got to it, he touched it with his toe and the baby crumbled into a pile of powder that the breeze picked up and scattered like ashes.

"Thank you," the girl whispered.

Jarrod put his head against the girl's warm stomach. She put her hand on the back of his head and ran her fingers through his hair.

"I've missed a lot of sleep thinking about what happened to that baby," the girl said. "I've had me some terrible dreams. That the baby's in a fishing net somewhere getting slapped by big silver fish. Or that it's just bobbing around like a plastic doll. Sometimes I stay in the tub too long and my feet wrinkle up all soft and white and I imagine the baby maybe just melted away. Like tissue paper left out in the rain."

Jarrod opened his eyes. He turned to look at the girl.

"There it is!" she said with a sudden smile. "I felt it take inside! I think we made a baby!" She hugged her knees closer and Jarrod reached out gentle to her face. "You don't have to come back no more. We did what we set out to do."

Jarrod felt something in him give way just as the sand on the dune had as the horse descended. A whole shelf of something broke loose in him and he couldn't gather it back up. "We better make sure," he said. "I'll come back again."

The girl let her knees down and turned off the horse lamp. "That ain't necessary," she said. "Now I'm going to take a nap and let the baby cook."

"What's your name?" Jarrod asked in the cold dark.

"Marie," the girl said.

Then Jarrod rose and dressed in the darkness. He stood for a while in the cold room and listened to the girl breathe. Then he let himself out of the house.

*

That night, the moonlight came through Jarrod's window as bright as sunlight. He couldn't sleep, so he got up and found a hammer and some nails and nailed up a quilt over his window. But still, the light came in around the corners, so Jarrod rose a second time and found a roll of duct tape, and he taped the quilt to the wall as best he could, but still, the light found a way in through the quilt's stitching. Jarrod lay on his back and squeezed his eyes closed. He and the girl were on the orange horse, but the horse had turned from a real horse back into a ceramic one and he and the girl were sliding, sliding off its slick back.

In the morning, Jarrod went to his first service call. While he adjusted the satellite, he saw himself pulling weeds from the perimeter of the girl's rental. He saw himself kneeling at the girl's feet, painting her toes the same tangerine color of the horse lamp. After Jarrod got the satellite working, he called in sick for the rest of the day and drove himself to the girl's house. On the stoop, he felt weak and out of sorts from the heat and lack of sleep, but he knocked and knocked until a long-haired guy, shirtless and sleepy-eyed, opened the door.

"You better not be selling anything," the guy said. "I got enough cookies and God." Behind the guy, Oreo rose with some struggle. He staggered to the door and peeked through the guy's knees and thumped his tail when he saw Jarrod.

"I'm friends with your roommate," Jarrod said. "I came to talk to her."

"Penny's not here," he said. "She's gone."

"I'm not looking for Penny," Jarrod said. "I'm looking for Marie."

The guy raised one foot and bent his knee and pushed backwards on Oreo's snout with his heel. "No Marie lives here," he said. "You got the wrong place."

Jarrod said nothing. He watched Oreo retreat from the foyer and lie down, hard and fast like he'd been shot. "She had red hair," Jarrod finally said. "Crooked teeth."

The guy nodded. "That's Penny," he said. "The liar. You can come in and see for yourself that she ain't here."

The guy opened the door and motioned inside and Jarrod came in. Oreo got up in pained loyalty and nosed Jarrod in the crotch. "She even left her goddamn dog," the guy said. "What am I going to do with a goddamn dog?"

Jarrod felt more sand fall away from the dune inside him. Shelf after shelf broke free. He went down the long, narrow hall with the guy and the dog at his heels and when he got to the door, he paused with his hand on the plastic gold doorknob and squeezed his eyes shut and he saw nothing.

"Go on," the guy said. "I don't have all day." Jarrod took a deep breath and turned the knob. "I mean, I do have all day," the guy said. "But this ain't how I planned on spending it."

Inside, the room was as bright as a cathedral. The sun poured in the single window and the walls were so drenched in light they didn't even look pink. On the floor, the mattress was bare. The clothes were gone and the towels were gone and the foil-wrapped TV was gone. All that remained was the little horse lamp and Jarrod went over to it and kneeled.

"Penny was a mess," the guy said. "Always will be."

Jarrod clicked the lamp on and clicked the lamp off. In the bright white of the day, he couldn't tell a difference between the two. He unplugged the lamp and wrapped the cord around it and stood.

"Take it," the guy said. "It's yours."

Jarrod clutched the lamp to his chest and pushed past the guy and past the thumping dog and ran out into the day. In the van, he sat for a long while, panting, working to catch his breath, working to convince himself that he didn't have a problem, but that he'd solved one. On the dashboard, more pollen had collected like blown sand. When he could finally breathe normally, Jarrod took the horse lamp off his lap and placed it next to him on the bench seat. He put it right in the middle, like a child placed between the two people who had made it.

BJORN

B Y THE TIME Bianca turned twelve, there had been twelve
doctors in total. If Bianca's mother had had her way, there
would have been twelve hundred. The only reason her
mother stopped with the doctor train was because Bianca's father
threatened to leave, with his wallet, if she continued. Still, Bianca's
cyst was her mother's whole life, and Bianca's mother's obsession
with the cyst was Bianca's whole childhood.

The cyst protruded from Bianca's forehead in a way that was
hardly noticeable to most people but caught the light in a way that
was always noticeable to Bianca's mother.

"It looks like you've run into a door," her mother would say,
squinting at Bianca's hairline. "Like you've given yourself a goose
egg. I'm afraid people think you're clumsy."

*

Eleven of the twelve doctors said the same thing to Bianca and her
mother: "It's a dermoid cyst. There's really no reason to remove it."

The twelfth doctor said the same plus some. "It's what we call
a 'vanished twin.' It never developed in *your* womb," he pointed to
Bianca's mother, "so *your* forehead absorbed it," he pointed to Bianca.

The doctor leaned his face so close to Bianca's as he made this pronouncement that she could smell what he'd had for lunch—Italian sub. "It's nothing to fret over. I see these all the time." He scribbled something on a prescription pad and handed it to Bianca's mother. "There's no need for surgery unless it turns problematic. Now scoot, young lady! Live your life!"

In the car, Bianca's mother wept. Bianca hoped it was because her mother was blaming herself, but she knew it was because the doctor had deemed neither the cyst, nor Bianca, problematic. Bianca tried to remember a time her mother had looked her in the eye and not at her forehead, but she could not think of a time like that. As they drove out of the parking lot, Bianca pulled the prescription from her mother's purse. "Get bangs!" was all it said.

That night, Bianca read in an old encyclopedia that dermoid cysts produced their own hair and teeth and fingernails. In the accompanying color illustrations, she saw dissected cysts that she knew she would never forget. Some of them looked like beefsteak tomatoes cut open and jammed with cat fur and seed pearls. That day, Bianca saw herself for what she really was: a host for a monster.

*

When she went away to college, Bianca finally followed the twelfth doctor's orders and cut thick bangs to hide the cyst. She began sleeping with whomever, wherever. Boys, girls, teachers. Beds, floors, bleachers. Her efforts worked until they didn't. By sophomore fall, a recurring nightmare had begun. Desperate and haunted, Bianca went to see the campus psychologist.

"I have this dream that a baby hatches from my temple," Bianca said, quietly and ashamed. "It's my long-lost brother, and my father is the happiest I've ever seen him."

The counselor put a hand over his mouth and cleared his throat. Both gestures, Bianca could tell, hid his amusement. She was so humiliated, she never went back—to the counselor or to school. For a week, she slept in her car. She cried and cursed and cradled her forehead. On the eighth day, she bought the webcam and rented the furnished apartment. On the ninth day, she began undressing for strangers on the internet. She made no attempt to hide her identity, only her forehead, and with the money she earned, she had necessities delivered to her front stoop: soup and toilet paper and tampons, lipstick and push-up bras and thongs.

For months, Bianca didn't leave her apartment for any reason or person or thing. She kept the blinds drawn and let her skin turn the color of skim milk. She sent her parents a postcard telling them she had left school for a stable job and that she didn't know when she would see them next. Bianca knew her mother was frantic. Not because she wanted to see Bianca, but because she needed to see the cyst.

*

Bianca did not go home for Christmas, but she did send her parents a gift box of twelve Royal Verano pears. They cost her fifty dollars, but they were perfect. On the internet, Bianca zoomed in on the pears and knew her parents would approve; they were nestled in their padded crates like one dozen flawless foreheads. She had them shipped certified mail so her parents would have to sign for them.

On New Year's Eve, she found a life coach online and spent three hours messaging about her cyst and her nightmare. The life coach told Bianca that she suffered from a classic case of "survivor's guilt," and that she needed to start calling the cyst what it really was: *her brother.*

"Have you even named him?" the life coach asked. "Because you need to give him a name."

Bianca thought about this. She thought about what sort of name went with Bianca. *Bianca and Ben? Bianca and Brian? Bianca and Bill?* "Bjorn," Bianca said at last. "Bianca and Bjorn."

The life coach was quiet for a pause, and Bianca could tell this choice pleased her. "Excellent," the coach said. "Now. Go and write your brother's story. Start a journal. Get to know Bjorn. Learn to love him."

*

Getting to know Bjorn was harder than the life coach had made it sound. Bianca tried to think of what her brother might have looked like and what he might have been able to do. She gave him red hair and green eyes and put him in a cowboy outfit. She tried to imagine him firing two cap guns and wearing a coonskin cap. She gave him a toy drum and a bullwhip and other things she had seen little boys use on old-fashioned television shows, but as soon as she'd written these things down, she scribbled through them. Bianca knew the truth. She knew Bjorn was weak, terribly so, because she had overcome him in the womb. Bianca could barely open a new jar of strawberry jelly, so what did that say about her brother? It said that if her brother had been born, he would have worn thick glasses and hearing aids and braces on his legs. He would have been unable to control his saliva, his bowels. He would have garnered the pity of her parents even more than he did now.

Bianca filled two notebooks on this predicament—on Bjorn's endless doctors' appointments and the exorbitant medical bills and the tears her parents shed for him and only him. She wrote all of this at her bedroom window and allowed herself to crack the blinds while she did so. Through the aluminum slit, Bianca could see into the neighbors' backyard. They had a rusted, metal seesaw with faded red-and-white candy stripes, and as she wrote about her brother's condition, she saw herself, and him, on the seesaw. She saw him on one end of it, tiny and malformed and high in the air. And she saw herself on the other end of it, staring up at her brother, his fate in her weight. Every time she looked at the seesaw, Bianca saw this, and then she saw herself getting up and off the seesaw and walking into the woods, while Bjorn crashed and fell.

*

The cyst began to grow. It grew so much that Bianca had to order a wig and undress at certain angles for her webcam customers. She lost a dozen subscribers because she wouldn't lay back and moan like she once had. If she did, her bangs fell to one side and she could feel the stale apartment air wafting over her cyst. She knew the men weren't looking at her forehead, but still: knowing it was exposed made her self-conscious and she couldn't do what she had once done as well as she once had.

The nightmare also grew worse. Now it was no longer a baby that hatched right from her temple. Now it was a full-grown man dressed as a Navy pilot. He stepped out of Bianca's head in his shined shoes, and her mother and father ran, tear-stained and rejoicing, to embrace him.

Bianca knew the time had come for action. But action meant leaving the apartment, so she found someone on the internet who would come to her and do what needed to be done.

*

Bianca didn't know if he was a real doctor or not, but he arrived when he said he would and he gave the secret knock that Bianca had insisted he use. More importantly, he carried a black leather bag that looked expensive and he didn't smell like an Italian sub. In Bianca's living room, the doctor put on surgical gloves and a head-lamp and asked Bianca to lay on the couch. Then he brought out five giant needles, two Valium, a scalpel, and a CD player. "Vivaldi," he said. "*Four Seasons*." He handed Bianca a blindfold and she put it on and the doctor did what she had paid him to do. When it was over, he helped Bianca to a seated position and held up a mirror so she could look at herself.

"I look like Frankenstein," she said of the stitches.

The doctor snapped off his gloves and smiled. "He's my favor-ite monster."

At Bianca's request, the doctor let her keep the cyst. He handed her an opaque jar filled with formaldehyde and suggested she not open it. "Dermoid cysts aren't much to look at," he said. "Just put the jar on your bookshelf and use it as a bookend." Bianca nodded and pretended she would. Then she wrote the doctor a check for all the money she had.

That night Bianca slept better than she'd ever slept. She dreamed there was a hole in her head and that a white dove flew into the hole and then the hole closed up like it had never even been there.

*

In the first week after the surgery, Bianca went around her apart-ment and opened all the blinds. She lay on her bedroom floor in a square of sunshine and smiled as her skin turned from skim milk to heavy cream. In the second week, Bianca went and stood on the front stoop and waved at passing cars. In the third week, she put on a hat to cover her bandage and walked two blocks to the gas station.

She bought Fig Newtons and beer and made small talk with the cashier about the weather. When she returned to her apartment, she went inside to put five beers in the refrigerator, then she promptly came back out with one beer and the cookies. She went into the neighbor's backyard and sat on one end of the rusted seesaw. She sat there in the yellow, late-winter grass and drank her beer and ate her cookies and looked up at the empty end of the seesaw in the blue sky and was happy.

In the fourth week, Bianca opened the jar in the kitchen sink. She rinsed the cyst under running water and set it out to dry on a tea towel. It looked like a raw chicken breast but darker—maybe a duck breast—and when Bianca cut into it, she could see the red hair she'd assigned Bjorn, plus a row of tiny teeth, a weak attempt at a smile she'd taken away. When she was done looking at it, she put the cyst back in the jar and put the jar back on her bookshelf so it could go back to doing its job.

*

Bianca ordered a half dozen Royal Verano pears for herself. When they arrived, she held them up to her face in the mirror and compared them to her new forehead. They were like six little twins and she loved them so much that she ate five in one sitting. Afterward, she slept for a long time and dreamed the dream of the dove. When she woke, she went and got the jar from the bookshelf. She opened it in the sink and poured off the formaldehyde and rinsed the cyst as she had before. Then she wrapped it in a tea towel and packed it in the padded Royal Verano crate and drove to her local veterinarian.

"He was born the same day I was," she told the vet, handing him the crate.

The vet was solemn. "You must be devastated."

"I don't know how I feel," said Bianca.

The doctor took the crate gently. "Give yourself time," he said.

Bianca said she would. She went back to her apartment and looked at herself in the mirror. She arranged her bangs to hide her stitches, then she turned on her webcam.

*

When Bianca went to pick up the ashes from the vet, she realized the urn she'd bought was too big. The ashes only filled a small envelope, but Bianca took the envelope home anyway and folded it into the urn and glued the urn's lid shut. The urn was painted blue and white and featured a girl and a boy at a wishing well. The boy was just standing there while the girl brought up the pail. Bianca tested the urn's lid to make sure it was secure, then she went to the kitchen and boiled an egg. When it was cool, she placed it on her forehead where the cyst had been. She wrapped a scarf over the egg and around her head, but she wasn't satisfied with how she looked. She wanted the cyst to be bigger. She wanted her mother to be horrified, more defeated than ever. So, Bianca rummaged through the kitchen until she came across the last Royal Verano pear in the back of the refrigerator. She placed the cold twin against her head and wrapped her head with the scarf. Bianca looked in the mirror and approved.

Later that night, when her parents opened their front door and saw Bianca on the stoop, Bianca's mother gave an audible gasp. She put her hands over her mouth and shook her head violently.

"Here," Bianca said, holding out the urn. "I brought you something for your trouble."

Bianca's father took the urn. Her mother cried like she had after the twelfth doctor visit, the one where neither Bianca nor the cyst had been deemed problematic.

"We were just going to eat," her father said. "Won't you join us for dinner?"

Bianca said she would. She set the urn in the center of the table. They ate in silence while her father stared at his plate and her mother stared at the cyst and Bianca stared at the urn.

When it was time to leave, Bianca put her hand on her forehead and said, "Thank you for dinner, but we really must get going."

*

Bianca moved to a new town. She threw out her webcam and thongs and push-up bras and grew out her bangs. She let her skin turn from white to pink to tan. She began a new career as a life coach and told everyone the same thing no matter what their problem was: that they felt guilty about being alive and needed to write letters to the dead.

On dates, over steak and wine, or duck breast and beer, she always told the men the same thing: that she didn't want children because she'd already lost one. She would describe the seesaw and the accident and the death. She would describe the cremation—how few ashes there were, because the child had been so small—and she would describe the blue-and-white urn, how she'd chosen it, how the girl painted on it pulled the bucket up from the well while the boy just stood there. Men never asked Bianca out again, but she didn't care. She always sent a crate of Royal Verano pears to thank them for their time. She wasn't looking for love. She just wanted to tell the story, her story, over and over again. It was a story that grew with each telling, that developed with each new detail. Sentence by sentence, cell by cell, the story emerged and enlarged. Until it was larger than Bianca. Larger than life.

ACKNOWLEDGMENTS

I am indebted to a host of midwives who helped deliver this beast baby of a book. Endless thanks to the brilliant Sarabande team of Sarah Gorham, Jeffrey Skinner, Kristen Renee Miller, Emma Aprile, Joanna Englert, Danika Isdahl, Alban Fischer, Natalie Wollenzien, and Lacey Trautwein; the Spalding MFA gurus Sena Jeter Naslund, Kathleen Driskell, Lynnell Edwards, Karen Mann, Katy Yocom, Ellyn Lichvar, and Jason Hill; my many beloved teachers, particularly Penny Lastinger, Ann Eames, Geoff Marchant, Bill Rosenfeld, Margaret Price, Leslie Daniels, Robin Lippincott, Pete Duval, Neela Vaswani, and Rachel Harper; and the kind people and publications who/that took an early chance on me, notably Michelle Dozois, Kurt Luchs, Lauren Passell, Greg Olear, *McSweeney's Internet Tendency*, *New Limestone Review*, *Grist*, and *The Pinch*.

Above all else, I am grateful for the love and support of my family and friends, especially my parents Ginger and Dan, my sister Liz, my bestie Tori, my literary life raft Donna Gay, my writing buds Amanda Burr Xido, Clint, and Natalie, my indispensable Lexington and Lakeville women, my late loved ones, my gracious God in Her many forms (new plotlines and old trees, to name the top two), and—most of all—Robbie, George, and Mark.

The stories in this collection were previously published by the following literary magazines:

Moon City Review, "The Nest"

The Southeast Review, "Sunday" (originally titled "Disarmed")

The Gateway Review, "Big Bad," Editor's Choice Award

Ninth Letter, "Drawers"

The Pinch, "The Entertainer," 2020 Pushcart Prize Winner

New Limestone Review, "Daddy-o"

Grist, "The Pupil," 2020 Pushcart Prize Special Mention

Quarter After Eight, "Stone Fruit"

Solidago Journal, "Three Couches"

Pamplemousse, "Lonelyhearts" (originally titled "Ms. Lonelyhearts")

Raleigh Review, "Good Guys"

The Laurel Review, "The Horse Lamp"

Shirley Magazine, "Bjorn"

WHITNEY COLLINS received a 2020 Pushcart Prize, a 2020 Pushcart Special Mention, and won the 2020 American Short(er) Fiction Prize. Her stories have appeared in Catapult's *Tiny Nightmares* anthology, *American Short Fiction, AGNI, Slice, Shenandoah, New Ohio Review, Ninth Letter, The Southeast Review, Grist, The Pinch,* and *The Chattahoochee Review,* among others. She received her MFA from Spalding University and lives in Kentucky with her family.

SARABANDE BOOKS is a nonprofit literary press located in Louisville, KY. Founded in 1994 to champion poetry, short fiction, and essay, we are committed to creating lasting editions that honor exceptional writing. For more information, please visit sarabandebooks.org.